# THE REVELATION GATE

To Dad —

Thanks again.

B. blessed

Gen. 12:1-2

# THE REVELATION GATE

BRIAN L. THOMPSON

ISBN: 978-0-615-44374-4

Library of Congress Control Number: 2011921475

# ACKNOWLEDGEMENTS

To: My Lord and Savior Jesus Christ, who continues to provide the gift, ideas and inspiration to write.

My wife, #1 fan and business partner Heather, and my daughter Zae. Thank you for sacrificing family time to let Daddy write away in his dungeon!

My parents, Bradley and Barbara, for their undying love and support.

My focus group members, especially Nakia Brown. I appreciate the honest criticism, brainstorming and ideas.

My editor and brother in Christ, Steven Manchester, and my friend Jeff Ransom for the history lesson.

The support system of friends, family members, and accountability partners that make Great Nation Publishing work.

Last, but not least, my pastor and spiritual father, Bishop Eddie L. Long.

Watch for my next novel, *The Anarchists*, due in 2012.


*Tazama Mkombozi!*

*This work is dedicated to the memories of*

*Martia Logan, Kayla Ward, and Alex Pace,*

*who remind me to love in the present*

*and cherish the importance of the moment.*

# CAST OF CHARACTERS (in alphabetical order)

Adui wa EL: One of the gods in the Otī pantheon; the lone god of the *Kusini mwa watu*

Aitan, *Uché scribe; father to Chimelu*

Auni, *an Uché cleric and hermit*

Bimnono, *mother of Lusala, third wife of Aitan*

Chimelu, *son of Isoke*

EL, *the Uché god*

Fola, *older brother of Isoke*

Gamba, *son of Aitan and Mairi*

Hawa, *an Uché seer who suffers occasional bouts of dementia, mother of Fola and Isoke*

Isoke, *mother of Chimelu; second wife of Aitan afflicted with a blood disorder*

Kabal, *chief guardsman of Kgosi, then Kgosi II*

Kaizari Amiri Jeshi Mkuu, *Emperor of the known realm*

Kgosi, *king of the Otī*

Kgosi, II (also called "Muuaji"), *son of Kgosi and his successor*

Letsego, *Uché scribe; older brother of Aitan*

Lusala, *daughter of Aitan and Bimnono*

Madiha, *second daughter of Aitan and Mairi*

Mairi, *first wife of Aitan*

Mkombozi, *"The Deliverer" of the Uché people*

Mlinzi, *warrior herald of EL*

Mosi, *first king of the Uché*

Penda, *concubine to Kgosi and Kgosi II*

Sakina, *first daughter of Aitan and Mairi*

Sifa, *wife of Kabal*

Zarek, *fallen herald of EL*

# PROLOGUE

**N**ear the dawn of recorded time lived Mosi, the first king of the Uché people. Adored by his people, he ruled peaceably until committing an offense against EL, the god of the Uché. For this, EL divided Mosi's kingdom into northern and southwestern portions and handed it to two invading enemies – thus, beginning the Uché captivity.

The former belonged to a brave military leader of the Sanguë: a race of mixed Uché and Otī blood hailing from the unexplored regions. He ordered footmen to kill only as a last resort. Mosi, his wives, children and eleven brothers were spared. Known as "the eleven," these men were *clerics*: guardians of Uché history and liaisons between the people and EL. Kind but firm, the ruler of the north permitted his foreign captives relative freedom.

The latter territory fell to a political dilettante whose reign was marked by cruelty and bloodshed. He was of the Otī, a mountainous race originating from beyond the Great Mountain. Forceful and violent, the southwestern king sentenced dissidents to death. The Uché and Otī beneath him followed in fear, knowing the slightest wrongdoing or just a capricious whim may result in their death. Naturally, he and the northern ruler saw eye-to-eye on nothing, further defining the stark territorial division and raising the threat of conflict between the two.

After charming the royal courtiers to see his point-of-view, one night, under the auspices of consolidating the two kingdoms peaceably, the southwestern king assassinated his adversary and heirs as they slept. When dawn broke the next day, both the Sanguë and Uché populaces awoke to the bodies of the respected king and his bloodline paraded through the main streets.

Thereafter, the kingdoms united and their new ruler eliminated any natural successor to the throne – including his father, brothers, and own sons – to assume dictatorial control. He also destroyed Mosi and his family;

all but the eleven. These men were masters of *Njia* – an invisible power that gifted its masters with unnatural abilities. Shortly after the coronation, these men used their powers to infiltrate the palace in broad daylight. After dismissing the royal guard, the eleven confronted the king, who threw himself down from a window rather than face condemnation.

The overthrow struck fear into the hearts of the Otī and Sanguë. *If eleven men possessed enough power to rid themselves of the king, what could stop a fully empowered people?* With no direct successor to the throne, a high-ranking official in the Otī royal court became king. He immediately issued a directive to raze EL's temple and leave no cleric alive. The ensuing battle lasted nine days, ending with the building's sack and burning. All that remained were the eleven. Severely weak from fighting, Mosi's brothers endured atrocities before their execution.

Following his conquest, the new king discovered legislating for all three races was an overbearing task, so he appointed a regent over the Sanguë and relocated them across the District River. Still, the Uché presented a problem. Though he determined not to enslave them in the traditional sense, they could not be allowed certain freedoms – especially to follow *Njia*. Anticipating the move, Mosi's relatives exiled themselves and renounced it. Prior to their demise, the eleven predicted a New Order that EL would establish through Mosi's bloodline. In time, the Otī king hunted the Uché king's living relatives and exterminated them all.

But Anisa, a secret Sanguë concubine of Mosi, bore a son, Ijara, whose descendants bore sons over 700 years down to Jahleel, whose wife bore him Kifimbo. Kifimbo was the father of Aitan, the husband of Mairi, Isoke, and Bimnono. . .

# PART ONE

# ONE

## THE FIRST FULL MONTH OF HARVEST, 799 A.C.

❝ *Mkombozi* is soon to come."

Those reciting the history – the men too old or weak to work the ground – concluded it with that mantra. Their fathers and grandfathers had done so, and so on. However, by the present time, eras past the captivity, the phrase became trite and assumed a customary status similar to that of the greeting: "Be well and I will see you, if the sun so chooses to wake."

Only strict followers of EL gave *Mkombozi* much thought, except to superstitiously invoke his name during the flood season; for EL's emotions showed in weather changes. Turbulent storms indicated testing, or his displeasure. During those times, the Uché quieted themselves and respected the heavenly work. Calm weather meant he neither laughed nor wept, so they engaged in normal business.

But a plentiful rainy season, during which the District River flooded, indicated a good harvest and divine pleasure. Thus, they reveled in it – especially when holy rain fell; golden, sweet smelling, heavy dropping precipitation. It had been foretold that the birth of *Mkombozi* would occur at such a time. A direct blood descendant of their great warrior king, *Mkombozi* would travel to the realm's end to reestablish order.

Armed with the hope of birthing him, the unmarried, old or young exposed their bellies openly at suspect-looking precipitation. Unplanted and barren fields yielded significantly larger harvests than that of the fertilized areas after holy rain. Terminal and crippling diseases reversed themselves after holy rain. Its possibility encouraged the hopeless not to completely abandon belief in the metaphysical or *Njia.*

This strange behavior intrigued Kgosi. By contrast, the Otī and Sanguë believed in whatever they deemed meant them good at the time; a system of exchange he respected and followed. Regardless, he tolerated the foreigners' devotion because it kept them docile. His father once did the same for a similar reason. But one unknown detail persisted in troubling his sense of reason: *What benefit do they receive for their worship?* He must know it, as logic did not drive this confusing culture's devotion.

One day, to gain this understanding, he ordered the lone member of the clerical order to immediately enter into his presence.

According to tradition, to become a cleric, one must be of blood relation to Mosi. Since the purge hundreds of years ago, none stepped forward to accept the mantle, as doing so marked them for death. But Auni, hailing from a different lineage, claimed a divine call from EL to join the order – a request to which the king did not object.

Since then, he had constructed a makeshift temple and lived a hermetic existence inside of it, subsisting on animal and produce remaining from burnt sacrifice, as well as insects during poor harvests. His duties included service for up to half a flood season in the temple's inner sanctum, where the Uché believed that he communicated face-to-face with EL. That time now approached.

Therefore, when Kgosi called, Auni ceased preparations, grudgingly sent for one skilled in the Otī tongue and headed toward the palace. Upon his arrival at the throne room's entrance, a pair of massive hands gripped his shoulders and that of his translator, pushing them downward underneath the gold-inlaid doorframe. Both Auni and his translator locked their knees and refused to show respect to the king, whom the Otī believed to be a god fit to be worshipped on bended knee. According to the Uché, bowing before anyone but EL equated idolatry.

"Kneel." The chief royal guardsman, a rebel Uché

renamed Kabal, muttered through gritted teeth in Auni's language, "or I will cut off your feet so you have no choice."

"Then I will hobble on stumps," Auni retorted. "But I will not bow."

Kgosi extended a heavily-jeweled scepter toward the trio, clearing them to come forward. "Let him be. A modicum of pride is all they have. Permit them that."

"But my king, if we let *this one* get away with it, there will be others later."

"I have spoken for you to leave him be," he hissed. "Come forth, *prophet*."

The turncoat Uché released Auni, who walked the royal purple carpet, streaked a dark rust color and crusted with the clotted blood of slain dissenters. Though the translator looked down, Auni faced the ruler eye-to-eye. It was another protocol misstep. Lower social classes could not engage in direct eye contact with royalty.

"I will forgive your ignorance. . .*this time only*. Speak."

"Gracious king, you ask that I explain *Njia*. If it pleases you, I will answer."

The translator repeated the phrases verbatim, minus Auni's irreverent vocal inflection on "gracious."

"Speak then, of this religion."

"We are an imperial people not of this place, and. . ."

Kgosi interrupted. "You do not originate from this region?"

"EL is not of this realm and neither are we. We were created by the holy rain."

The court erupted with raucous laughter. Kgosi finally regained composure himself after the others stifled themselves. "That explains much, for now. I know you and your entire race to be strange looking *and* crazed. Created by *rain*, you say?"

"*Njia* is not a religion, but a belief in another realm, where EL is in absolute power and we, as his local regents, rule in authority. In believing this, we are able to manipulate the natural and achieve the impossible."

Kgosi stroked his beard, as the translation rolled forth. "Impossible abilities?"

"Moving objects with a thought," Kabal interjected. "Perceiving the thoughts of others. Some are believed to alter the composition of liquids and solids. Others increase the potential of an object until it is forced to replicate itself."

"Continue."

"Our prophets knew these things and more," said Auni, "but *Mkombozi*, the final cleric, is yet to come. A holy rain will arrive during the flood season. At that time, a woman vessel will be selected to bear him. He, the Son of Mosi, shall possess unbreakable bones, enter the Revelation Gate and usher us into a New Order. All will be restored and we shall reign here in this realm with *Mkombozi* as our king. None of this can you prevent."

"And where, or what, is this *Revelation Gate?* Tell me, so that I may see it."

"No one knows, Master," Kabal interjected. "It is a *myth*. No one knows what it is for certain. It is the subject of a tale they tell their young at night. *Someday, our hero will enter the Revelation Gate, establish a new kingdom and soar the skies like a bird.*" He flapped his arms like wings in scorn, drawing snickers. "Perhaps it is that door over there? Or there? It is a door to nowhere!"

"It is a tale you once loved," said Auni, drawing a scowl.

"This refuse is what your foreign god teaches you?" chuckled Kgosi to his magicians. "Madness is the only explanation. Why else deprive oneself of life's pleasures to indulge in poverty and misery? EL is a compassionate being who shackles his people to be oppressed for a millennium. Nonsense!"

"*He* did not shackle us," Auni shouted with indignation too quick for his translator to keep pace. "Neither did your father, whom you had murdered for the throne. Mosi's desecration brought us under subjection. No Otī effort alone. . ."

"Then we are grateful to Mosi! If this theory of yours proves correct, hermit, I, a living god, will be overthrown . . . by a *mythical* being who is the descendant of a long dead king. Will Mosi rise and produce an heir from the dust in which he now lies?"

"Await and you shall find out."

Horrified for his life, Auni's translator bit his tongue. After translating Auni's threat to the king, Kabal stepped from his place at the throne and drew his blade. "Say the word."

Kgosi's eyes bulged wide with fury. "Why bother? Take these fools from my presence." The guards grabbed the two Uché at the elbows. "And let them worship and believe whomever or whatever they want. EL is no threat to me!"

A time later, in his quarters, Kgosi pondered the strange encounter with the hermit and his mention of the holy rain. Two years ago, the Uché territory, called Nozi experienced only what could be described as a phenomenon. He witnessed this. A small cloud settled in Nozi and pelted the entire area with drops the shade of his golden crown. Moments later, the cloud and its yield dissipated into thin air. During the following harvest, a massive increase in crop production occurred and next planting season, a cursory census revealed the male slave infant population surged 40 percent over the previous year. *Perhaps the holy rain means something after all?*

A concubine, the one with the unnaturally short menstrual periods, appeared at his bedroom doors. He indicated that she should come forth.

Baring her breasts, she sidled up to Kgosi on the bed. The 25-year-old Uché girl named Penda gave him the most pleasure of all his young brides and bedmates. But inside, he wondered if she had secretly gone to his young son, Kgosi II, who had long been sneaking licentious looks at the petite woman. A prince sleeping with the king's concubine would be a false claim to the throne. As she kissed Kgosi, the thought distracted him.

"Something wrong, my love?" Penda continued to peck a trail of kisses along the front of his shoulder until he seized her by the arms.

"Have you gone in to my son?"

Startled, Penda stuttered. "N...no. Not on my life, my lord!"

"If your witness is false, I will have your head before the sun rises!"

The conviction in his accusation frightened the girl. Though she grew to care for him like a legal wife, the king's paranoia flourished since he added Penda to the royal harem. He knew Kgosi II, a few years her senior, had cast glances her way and even whispered what he believed he could do to her that his father could not. But, unlike Kgosi, nothing about the devious prince remotely attracted her. "I have not slept with him, I swear it!"

"Then swear it by *his* name." If she did so, Kgosi knew that she did not lie.

Sweat formed at Penda's brow. "I swear it," she said, her voice quavering. "By Gamba."

Kgosi loosened his grasp and she began to relax. "Two years ago, do you remember the holy rain?"

"Before you brought me here," she gasped. "My brother was born then."

Kgosi's face shifted from curious to pensive.

"If you have a question, ask me, my lord. Let me reveal my heart."

"Your brother is *Mkombozi* then."

"*Mkombozi* is a legend conjured by the prophets and those hopeful that the spear and sword spared one in Mosi's line. Your guardsman Kabal is Uché also, is he not? Surely, he must have told you this before."

*I thought so*, Kgosi mused, *but how can I be sure?* "Your people believe in him?"

"Many trust in the *possibility* of him," she whispered

close to his ear. "And others use the name to describe their optimism. Do whatever it takes to ease your mind with this. But be warned, my love. . .others are looking to the acts of your hands. Your predecessors possessed the foresight to erase hope by eliminating the eleven. Any sign of unsteadiness may now inspire a widespread lack of confidence in your rule."

"Indeed! You have spoken well." Kgosi clapped his hands loudly twice. Two men opened the royal chamber's doors.

"Assemble the wisemen, magicians and scribes and prepare wax for my seal," he instructed. "And close the doors behind you."

"Yes, my lord." The men about-faced and obeyed.

Kgosi turned to his concubine, who lay back and waited.

Later that evening in the throne room, Kgosi consulted with his sycophants. They affirmed the theory that the Uché population be under stricter control measures – particularly the male infants – to eliminate the possibility of a man-savior. He agreed without argument and floated the possibility of mass male castration; but its consequences would be widespread and devastating.

"According to their prophecy," the king thought aloud, "this future king is all but *invincible*."

One of the magicians asked for permission to speak, which Kgosi granted. "Oh great king, live forever! The prophet said his life must begin during a holy rain, and the flooding will not occur for another three moons."

"The last holy rain fell two years ago. What is to say this savior does not live?"

"There is no possibility, your highness," Kabal claimed. "Do not let that girl influence you. May I suggest that we dispose of her? I have a suspicion that she. . ."

"My favorite concubine? No. Like you, she betrays her

own too often to be a spy, but if she proves different, I will allow you to do whatever you see fit with her."

He grinned. "Your counsel is wise."

"Let it be written. . .execute male Uché children two years in age or younger. Search the home of Penda's father. Spare no male Uché found to be close to that age. Each centurion must follow these orders exactly. Any showing signs of invulnerability should be turned over to me."

The men furiously inscribed the words across the papyrus. After reading it to indicate his satisfaction or displeasure, the king tore it into pieces. Horrified, the men dropped to their knees, pleading for forgiveness from whatever offense they had perpetrated.

"Let the law be changed," Kgosi said. "Spare no young Uché child, male or female. *Kill them all.*"

# TWO

## FIRST DAYS OF THE FLOOD SEASON, SEVEN MOONS AFTER THE INFANTICIDE, 800 A.C.

For the very first time, Bimnono felt selfish for putting herself ahead of her husband's second wife, Isoke. From the moment she jumped the broom with Aitan and the two women swept the house floor a year ago, she antagonized Isoke, who was four years her elder.

Isoke proved to be an easy target, for she was barren, sickly and Aitan did not love her. He desired Isoke for her domesticity and care for his daughters, Sakina and Madiha – children by Mairi, the *first wife*, and Isoke's best friend. Isoke wed Aitan only under bondage of a promise to Mairi. Inside, Isoke hoped that she and Aitan might eventually grow to love one another and Bimnono knew of this.

But, in four years of wedlock – unknown to the elder who married them, but obvious to all whom observed their interactions – he and Isoke did not touch each other intimately. The blood on their marriage sheets belonged to a calf that Aitan's older brother, Letsego, slayed for the reception. If publicly known, this treachery invalidated their marriage and would bring shame to Aitan, so Bimnono stayed silent. Because of this, she pitied Isoke enough to offer her every chance to be present for the holy rain, predicted to fall any day now. But she wanted it so badly for *herself* and the next holy rain had been forecast as the last of this generation. None could predict when the skies would break before the end of the flood season.

She continued washing the breakfast dishes, adjusting her stance to compensate for her bulging belly. The Sanguë remedies did nothing to help her drop excess weight, or ease the pain in her twice-swollen joints. The weight gain insulted her formerly lithe dancer's figure. She *could not* be pregnant. If so, her child could not be *Mkombozi*, for the holy rain had not appeared for him to be conceived by it.

Bimnono lumbered toward her rival's hut and burst through the door unannounced. "Go to the marketplace for us," she insisted. Trails of sweat soiled the front of her dress. "You will not miss the holy rain. I am sure of it."

Isoke turned from her needlework. "What makes it 'holy' to *you*? And how are you so sure? Do you think EL would let *Mkombozi* come through a half-breed?"

"Do you not know your own history? Mosi's beloved Anisa was Sanguë."

Isoke huffed. "And look what became of us because of it? You speak of things you do not understand."

"What is there to understand? Look, it is about a half-day trip. I cannot walk as quickly as you. I am tired and swollen. Plus, some of the foodstuffs *are* for you, as you do not eat *common food*. If you want supper for the next few days, I suggest you get going."

Bimnono had pushed her around long enough. "Is it not enough you keep the girls from seeing their father because he is busy pleasuring you? They have not seen him in a fortnight! Do you not have hired underlings for your little duties? Bother them instead with this."

"How sweet," Bimnono spat. "You think of those little demons with braids as yours. I suppose you'd have to, considering. . ."

Isoke shot Bimnono a dirty glance. "Watch it, witch."

"Because of all the healing men *you have* seen from here to the boundaries, we cannot *afford* 'underlings'. Aitan labors by candlelight because of the debt you cause trying to cure *your* illness. That is why *his children* do not see him. Now, go to the marketplace and pick up these things for us."

Isoke self-consciously glanced at the misshapen clots trapped beneath the skin on her shoulders. She did not want to return to the sick colony, but her period showed early signs of its advent. "You go instead. I must finish up my housework. Looks like you need to get up and exercise anyway."

"How dare you?"

"No mortal man predicts EL, you hateful. . ." Isoke composed herself. "Keep Aitan and his genitals for all I care, *mbwa mwitu*, but I am not missing my chance. I am the first wife and it is *mine* to give orders, not take them."

At that, Aitan poked his head through the hut's door. *Mbwa mwitu* in the common Uché dialect meant *wild dog*.

"Isoke, let her be." He accepted coins from Bimnono and handed them off to Isoke. "I stopped to eat, not for lip. Do not defy me. And you are *not* the first wife."

The reminder struck Isoke like a hard kick to the midsection. "My sister is gone, almost four years now. Why am I not the first wife?"

"I am not in the mood for your insolent questions or female games."

"But *you* let her terrorize me! You are so busy with her and your. . .doings. Sakina and Madiha have not seen you in a fortnight and. . ."

"It will not take long," he interrupted. "It is the beginning of the flood season, not the end. If you see the sign of the holy rain on your way, turn around, but if not, continue on. Again, do not defy me. I will go by and look in on them."

Seeing a small cloud from a distance over the area might be tricky in the blazing sun. "Have the children watched by their grandmother until I return."

From there, Isoke proceeded at a brisk pace, stopping only to sip water from the animal skin hanging at her side. Leaving Nozi's "safe" confines worried her, especially after the mass slaughter of the young. Women had been known to be kidnapped by the Otī, only to reappear at the doorstep of their husbands – beaten, raped and, in some cases, missing a tongue. But the recent killing of infants proved to her that the Otī would do *anything* to anyone. The chaos and bloodshed during the ensuing riots heightened the enmity between the races. Logic dictated that Isoke go to the marketplace. She kept her peace and did not err from her duties while Bimnono might have lost a tongue over saying something stupid.

"Isoke!" At about the halfway mark between Nozi and the Otī territory, Letsego called out from a slow-moving chariot. "Isoke!"

"Blood!" she yelled in no particular direction. "Blood!"

"Since when have you known me to follow the ranting of a hermit?" he asked. "Besides, if I do not see proof, I do not believe it."

She pretended to ignore Letsego until he maneuvered the vehicle close enough for the horse's hooves to kick dust particles into her face. "Yes, Letsego, what is it?"

He pulled in the reins. "Allow me to escort you. The Otī will not bother you if we ride together. And with three bridled horses, you will be back in Nozi in no time."

"I am unclean," she protested. "Our laws forbid it and I adhere to them."

"Get in, and if it pleases you, I will not touch you."

Weighing a shorter trip against a lecture, Isoke boarded with reservation. Aitan's brother always surfaced whenever she least wanted him to. The animals trotted instead of galloped and she fought the urge to yank the straps herself. "If we are to proceed at this pace, I might as well have walked, brother. Make haste."

"There is time, dear Isoke. There is time." He paused. "The elders believe that the harvest will be bountiful and the peaches will be succulent. Will you prepare that delicious peach dish for me?"

Isoke closed her cloak, for Letsego spoke about fruit, but his intentions lingered upon her breasts. When she covered up, Letsego's eyes snapped to attention.

"If my husband requests it, then I shall prepare it. You may have some, as well."

He licked his lips. "Aitan will not request it, as his tastes differ from mine."

"Then have another prepare it. . .a maiden whose hand you seek."

He shook his head. "No. *You* must cook it for me. There is none like yours."

Isoke shuddered at his lurid suggestions and did not speak, even after he pulled over at the entrance to the Otī marketplace. She stepped out, bid Letsego leave, and firmly indicated that he should not tarry in anticipation of her return. When she returned, she intended to tell Aitan of his brother's advances, hoping that he would not dismiss them as harmless.

As Isoke entered the Otī territory, little activity took place. Recently, many who conducted trade invented reasons to go to Nozi during the flood season – hopefully, to experience the holy rain. Even foreigners were privy to its miraculous effects. Isoke's father, hardly a *mbwa mwitu* – although he acted as if he wanted to be – caught the last rain while drunk in an alley. He came home, free of the addiction to palm wine that drove him to ruin in the first place.

Later that night, Isoke envisioned herself giving birth to a blinding light. From that point on, she became a believer. It would take a mystical power like *Njia* to blot out her affliction and open her womb.

Weighed down by the foodstuffs slung over her back, she pressed on as fast as she could. *If it happens today, I cannot miss the chance*, she thought. *Walk faster.* She breathed steadily to keep the pain in her side from growing. No such fortune. *No time to waste.* She stumbled on an odd, copper-colored rock and her toes started bleeding onto her thongs. Without breaking stride, she altered her gait to ease the pain. Nozi's boundaries were in distant sight. She passed the point at which Aitan's brother picked her up. Sensing victory, Isoke removed the packages from her shoulder and retied her scarf to secure the loose locks that slipped onto her neck.

Just then, a cool sensation in the form of a light wind

and a drop of moisture dotted her sweat-dampened back. Tears poured forth from her eyes, as a tiny gray cloud floated overhead towards her destination. With the breeze at her back, Isoke dropped everything and broke into a flat sprint, hoping to catch enough of the living water to bring her light-bearing future to pass. Holy rain lasted long enough to accomplish its purposes – no more, no less.

As she closed in on the town, the cloud positioning itself and a steady golden downpour fell. Isoke ignored her body's signals to slow down and pushed toward the open northern gate. As sure as a faucet turning off from on, the downpour stopped seconds before she reached it. Not a lick of moisture remained. Isoke collapsed, gasped for breath and wept before the elders. Those whose wishes went unfulfilled surrounded her in a circle, sobbing. But no one dared touch her.

"Who is *she*?" one asked, as Isoke buried her face in the dirt.

"Looks like Aitan's wife," said another.

"Hmph," said Hawa, an elderly woman regarded as a seer. "Help her up."

Two of the men waited until Isoke stopped moving. They then lifted her up by the elbows. Hawa leaned in to see the face of her forlorn daughter, whom she no longer recognized.

"It is *you*," she whispered, loudly enough for only her and Isoke to hear. Hawa touched the young woman's forehead long enough for Isoke to buckle a bit at the knees. "You know where to go. And you will know what to do when you arrive there."

Still weak, Isoke obeyed her mother and trodded toward the eastern gates.

"Aitan!"

He jumped, his hand jarring the writing instrument

on the parchment. "You ruined my work. This law must be completed by sundown. It better be good."

"Your second wife returns," Letsego said with a twinge of excitement.

Incredulous, he cursed, grabbed a blank parchment roll and began writing. "Praise EL! And you disturbed me for *that?*

"She fell in the dirt near the gates. She may be injured."

*Isoke.* Disgusted, Aitan rumbled through the door to the building and met his wife, who now walked, her face marked with caked mud and pebble imprints.

"Where are my foodstuffs?" he demanded, roughly brushing off her face. "Dedicated food is expensive. And why were you on the ground? How dare you disrespect me carrying on like this?"

"I missed the last holy rain of my pitiful lifetime," she said in a despondent tone. "You and your foreign wife caused me to miss it."

Aitan grabbed her by the arm, but Isoke did not stop. "Will you not answer me? How dare you shame me looking like this?"

"You withhold me dignity by not touching me," she said, continuing to walk. "You deny me honor."

"I *will not* touch you," he said with disgust. "You are always *unclean.*"

"But I prepare your home, cook your meals and clean your dirty clothes," she continued. "Still, you give a *Sanguë* everything. Permit me to walk. Nothing more."

"And after you do." He loosened his grip. "You will return to me?"

"You will never hear my protests again."

"Go!" He unhanded her, pointed toward the eleventh hour sun and shouted loud enough for his co-laborers to hear. "Gather my foodstuffs and be home before the sun goes down, or I will whip you red myself!"

Isoke passed far beyond Nozi's gates until the stench of feces and stale urine offended her nostrils. She shifted her breathing back and forth between her mouth and nose, so she did not taste the scent or smell it long enough to lose her stomach. Invariably, she failed at one or the other and vomited three times before reaching the waste pits. There, a herd of swine buried themselves in the cesspools, picked out scraps, or rolled around in it.

Isoke's eyes caught a newer pit a few stone throws to the right. Full of a clear liquid, it completely overpowered the other pit's aroma the closer she drew to it. She dipped her finger in and licked it. With water's consistency, it tasted like honey and quenched all her thirst. Isoke cupped her hands, submerged them beneath the surface and splashed it against her face. Afterwards, her skin felt renewed and the drops that fell from her chin healed the gash on her bleeding foot.

The skies broke open with rain. Isoke welcomed it with open arms. *EL smiles upon me.* Hawa's instructions gained clarity, but Isoke could not swim. No one knew her location. *Who will come rescue me?* Without longer hesitation, she closed her eyes and leapt into the pool.

Near sundown, when Aitan arrived with Letsego, they discovered Isoke curled into a fetal position at its center. If it were not for Hawa, who claimed Isoke journeyed there to die, she very well may have died of exposure.

Letsego lifted the unconscious body from the belly of the dry pit, affixed ropes under its arms and called for Aitan to lift her to the edge.

"Shall she live?" Aitan panted.

"She is cold," said Letsego, while climbing out himself, "but breathing steady . . .very strong."

"Why is she not awake then?"

"I am not sure," said Letsego. "EL must be on her side, but should he be, considering what she set her mind to do?"

"She is still my wife, brother," said Aitan, pointing into

his chest. "Be careful with your words. Put her in the back and let us go."

Letsego frowned. "Where you cart animals? The jostling will injure her."

"Stay in back with her and I will drive!"

Letsego sat with his back to the cart, which allowed Isoke to rest comfortably against him. He welcomed the contact and enveloped Isoke with his arms at the waist – to secure her, of course. Aitan assumed as much when he looked back. His brother cared for Isoke; too much, sometimes, to be considered that of kin and not of a jealous suitor.

The fact that the marriage remained unconsummated pleased Letsego. He prepared the fraudulent blood on the wedding night with abundant vigor and helped them to continue perpetrating the façade without question. The attention Letsego paid her did benefit Aitan. If he ever perished, Letsego would not shirk the responsibility of caring for Isoke or even Bimnono, although neither one particularly cared for him.

*She will yet be mine*, he thought, granting her several kisses on the lips.

# THREE

## THE LAST DAYS OF HARVEST, EIGHT MOONS AFTER THE HOLY RAIN, 800 A.C.

*I* *have been healed!* The irregular flow of blood in Isoke's body ceased with the submersion in the holy rain. She initially doubted that the healing would last, for her menstrual cycle tended to revive when she least expected it. This sporadicity occurred for twelve years. At its longest, it lasted a week short of an entire moon.

Normally, mothers regarded it as a signal that the body had transitioned into womanhood. Hawa cursed it. No man tolerated a wife he could not sleep with, or whose duties went undone due to her presence in a sickness hut. Unlike Fola, a strong and healthy boy, Isoke would burden her parents for the remainder of her childbearing years. Until she became a seer and deserted her family, Hawa reminded her daughter of this shortcoming daily – as if Isoke possessed control over it. Though the young girl fought desperately against going away the first time, after two years of it, she grew somewhat accustomed to leaving her family for extended periods of time.

Since her 13th year, she alerted others to cover her responsibilities, packed clothes and tearfully departed – sometimes as late as the second watch of the night. If it happened at daytime, she shouted "Blood!" to warn others not to touch or approach her, as she was unclean by their law until the flow stopped for three straight days.

Now, not only had EL redeemed her of the blood, but he had gifted her with a *child! Beating softly inside my womb must be the heart of Mkombozi, for no other explanation exists!* She had not slept with a man in all of her 26 years, and the changes in her body corresponded with the night she obeyed Hawa's prophecy and laid down her life in the pit. Isoke did not remember anything of that time, outside of jumping into the water and being shaken awake by Aitan the following morning.

A moon afterward, the morning sickness began. Isoke passed it off to Aitan as a result of the blood condition. He did not question her further, as he preferred not to rattle her fragile state-of-mind. She continued to quarantine herself regularly with the similarly afflicted and pregnant women to avoid suspicion – particularly when the morning sickness struck its hardest. No one in the sick hut paid attention to the other unless it was to aid in childbirth. It was a skill Isoke did not possess. She observed it and mentally took note.

Keeping Aitan unaware of this expectancy was critical. According to Otī law, if Isoke birthed a male child, he must paint their doorframe with four diagonal strokes intersecting with a central line at two points. This signaled that a boy had been born there. A soldier would come to destroy him. Almost five years ago to the day, Aitan did so. Failing to comply with the law was an act of treason punishable by death – *but he did not have to do it so readily.* They barely had to hold out hands for the boy, whom, he claimed, was "too *weak* to be *Mkombozi.*" That night, Gamba dropped to the river bottom.

Soon thereafter, Mairi bound Isoke to that matrimonial promise and swore to the heavens she had heard the District River calling for an avenging. Isoke witnessed the downward spiral, starting with Mairi yanking out her own dreadlocks one by one until she was bloody scalped, and prattling on and on about how her son wanted retribution. The elders quarantined her to a special colony for the crazed outside of Nozi, from where Mairi mysteriously disappeared not much later. Sick with grief, Isoke did not sleep until she had scrubbed the house clean of that wretched five-lined symbol.

Now, as Isoke passed with a basket of freshly-washed sheets and underclothes bobbing on her head, the seers smiled. She respected them, though the gift of foreknowledge gradually eroded her mother's grip on reality. These men and few women perceived the truth of her condition, and recited daily what little they knew of the centuries-old prophecy. But, with most of the original texts lost in the destruction of the temple, the stories of deliverance seemed more myth than reality. If they were true, no one knew the location of the Revelation Gate or its nature. After all, to them, the ruling body of the entire known realm was unlikely to be overthrown by *one man.*

Isoke looked down, conscious of her expanded waist. Since her third moon of expectancy, she strapped down her swollen breasts with a leather belt. Fortunately, even through this – her eighth moon – her belly swelled just enough to pass off to her husband as extra weight. Bimnono had tried to do the same, but failed miserably. But he must not know of *this* child. If Aitan found out, he could have her stoned – though no adultery had been committed. In the early days, even she did not believe EL was responsible for this child, and it might well be a dream until she felt the kicking.

She dreaded the day of childbirth. For the past three nights since returning from self-imposed exile, Isoke experienced false pains and secretly slept with a towel between her teeth to muffle her cries. After waking up this particular day, she set about her morning routine: arranging breakfast, getting Sakina and Madiha ready for instruction and completing her daily chores. She made it through nearly the entire day without incident until her insides quaked with a contraction that dropped her to her knees. As the pins and needles subsided from the smack of her kneecaps against the dirt floor, a warm wetness surrounded her scraped skin.

Isoke rose and stumbled to the hearth before the next one hit. This one felt as if the bottom of her womb had ripped apart. Before she knew it, a wail escaped her lips. It was unlike a sound she had ever heard outside a funeral procession. Fortunately, it was the final day of harvesting. No one was around to hear it.

A few feet away, a clear puddle of fluid mocked her. It was as if it knew that Aitan, due to return from his scriptorium, would piece two and two together. Though her planned hiding place – the five-foot-deep cellar with an entrance in the girls' room – was only another lunge or two away, she hurried to the wet spot and patted the dirt floor dry with the outer fringe of her clothes. *My son's purpose is too great to lose on sloppiness.* The pain subsided long enough for her to climb undetected into the hole and lie on the steps. Descending further would immerse her in complete darkness.

Later, Aitan arrived, found his house tidy but dinner unmade, cursed his absent wife and left, just as she had hoped he would do. With the door now secured, the girls knew to go to their grandfather's hut, for no child in the village would dare be at home alone. Their parents would whip them red, if they disobeyed.

As the temperature in her shelter plummeted and her breath became visible, Isoke became aware of the hours that passed while she labored. Aitan would not stand for insolence from any wife of his. The sun had gone down and the children's grandfather may be displeased in having to keep the children extra long. *Aitan may beat me just for the thrill of it.* But she stood to lose more by interrupting the birth over temporary matters of inconvenience. Despite these things, Aitan and the girls would live tomorrow, and her *son* must do the same. Isoke buried her teeth in the bitter root in her mouth and pushed. She reached her hand between her legs and felt a moist clump of baby hair.

"Isoke!" Aitan's tired voice boomed from the front door. He unloaded a sleeping daughter from each shoulder onto the dinner pillows. "Isoke!"

Another push later and the head and shoulders were in proper position. She bit the root until it gave in the middle. *One more good push might do it.*

"You can stop keeping secrets. I know it *all.*"

Isoke shuddered and backed against the jagged wall.

"You have been cured and your womb curses me with the fruit of another's seed."

She positioned her left hand on her knee and her right beneath her son's emerging body.

"When it is born, boy or girl," he shouted, while entering Madiha and Sakina's room, "it will starve on the Great Mountain and be eaten by hyenas. The next day, birds will peck at your flesh and EL will judge and condemn your soul to *Kuzimu*."

Isoke unleashed a terrible scream and the ground shook, as if it were an earthquake.

"Father," a bleary-eyed Sakina yelled, "what's happening?"

A section of the hut's heavy ceiling dropped between them, stopping him cold. "Go!" He pointed to the wall beneath three wedding brooms. "Stay there!"

The structure shook at its foundation, sending clay plates and cups to the floor. Isoke's treasured blown glass trinkets followed. Sakina and Madiha shrieked with each resounding smash. Aitan backed against the wall beneath an overhang, shielding his head with his hands. In front of him, the earth parted open like a hungry child's mouth. Struggling to stand his ground, he audibly repented for his transgressions, one after the other, concluding with his most recent threats to Isoke. The tremors gradually subsided. As the girls held each other, rigid with shock, Aitan barely managed to sidestep the chasm in the earth.

"Girls," Isoke muttered. "Aitan? Do you live?"

Transfixed by the sight of their father, inches away from certain death, they wept and refused to move. He, too, did not budge. Isoke leveraged her rubbery limbs enough to maneuver back to the surface.

"Madiha, Sakina," she repeated, "Aitan. If you live, *come*."

Aitan edged a little toward the beckoning voice. Isoke lay propped up against the wall, with her new baby wrapped in torn off sections of her clothes. The unremarkable-looking child with plump cheeks cried a little and made a sucking noise. Madiha, who had just turned eight years old, took a natural interest in babies. "Father, it's a boy! What will you name him?"

"He shall be called *Chimelu*," Isoke said, "for he is made of our god."

Sakina, the eldest by two years, frowned. "Mama Isoke, what will we do? The Otī will seize him, as they take all boys!"

The announcement sent Madiha into hysterics. All she knew about the infanticide was the night that soldiers interrupted their sleep to search for young ones and the many moons of mourning that followed.

Aitan ordered the girls out of the room to fetch clean cloths, water and soap and stared intently at Isoke's newborn. "How can this be? You have given *another* a son." Aitan's statement quaked his inner being, as he could not produce a male heir, himself. He held a knife at his side and approached her. "To whom does this illegitimate belong? *I will have his head.*"

Without flinching, Isoke maneuvered her breast free, allowing her hungry son to suckle. "He is no illegitimate. His father is EL."

After slicing the umbilical cord and removing the afterbirth, which is not what Aitan originally thought to do, he broached the subject once more. "EL is Father to us all. The boy's father is my brother. I see how he looks at you and how he kissed you."

"He did not kiss me! If you paid attention, you have seen how I look back. I kissed and slept with no one – least of all Letsego." Her tone startled Chimelu, who stopped feeding and whimpered. "He was conceived by the holy rain. I was healed in this manner."

Aitan huffed. Even if that were true, it would not stop the Otī from coming for the boy. "You resort to legends and wild untruths? Fine, *I* will paint the mark on the hut. But you will tell me who this boy's father is – even if I must beat it from you."

The girls returned with the supplies and together, the couple cleaned the baby as he nursed.

"Sakina, take your sister into my room and play until I come to get you."

"Yes, Father." Although the two girls left the room, Isoke and Aitan kept their voices to harsh, combative whispers.

"You will do no such thing," Isoke said, "nor give him away, as you did to Gamba, your own flesh and blood. Do you not understand? He is *Mkombozi.*"

"There *is* no *Prophesied One.* Would you have all of us jailed for *your* scandalous indiscretions, or worse?"

"I do not wish anyone to suffer. Send us away to the land of the Sanguë, where the Otī do not rule. Bimnono may travel there freely and you can tell them that I perished in the moving of the earth."

Since the infanticide, the Otī prohibited outer-region travel by the Uché, whom they basically now enslaved. Violators were punished with whipping and, in some cases, fire branding or the loss of toes or a foot. Those found to have aided them received it just as badly. "The Otī *do* rule there. Their king is an Otī regent."

"Then, we will keep a low profile and only leave at night," she argued.

"The living nerve! You have yet to give me reasoning why you should not be stoned for your betrayal of our vow. You deceived me about your condition of blood, all this time. And you claim I should smuggle you to freedom!"

Isoke exploded. "Stubborn jackass . . .no one betrayed you! We must make haste, for he is *Mkombozi* and our last hope for freedom. If I am in error, then put me away in divorce, or stone me. You lose nothing but a servant. But if I prove correct, your stubbornness will result in the death of all!"

Aitan contemplated the request. "It cannot be so."

"Please! We will return to Nozi when EL permits. His favor is upon us. I swear it upon my life and the life of my son."

Surprised by her bravado, Aitan doubled back. "You are in no position to give commands or requests. Without any aid, you will not make it past Nozi's gates."

"Which is why I ask for your help. Come with us."

"I will not." He softened his stance. "Bimnono may escort you on this fool's errand, *if she wishes*. Sakina and Madiha stay. There is no sense in all of us perishing."

His convenient cowardice made sense. A fairly *affluent* chief scribe would be noticed missing more than that of two women. "As you wish."

"I will yoke cattle and she will hide you in an oxen cart." A little sympathy tinged his voice. "I will pad it so that you. . .and *him*. . .will be comfortable, and you will be sent for when the time has come and the danger has passed. May EL have mercy on your soul, if the Otī come to my doorstep for this."

She humbly assented. "You have spoken well."

"If you are caught, you know they will kill all of you."

"And if I remain," she retorted, "they will kill us both, for I will not let him die. I have little recourse. Let it be unto me, as you have said."

From there, the arrangements occurred quickly. While Aitan prepared and sealed the traveling papers, Isoke packed as much of her belongings as feasible and explained to her adopted daughters that they must not speak of her absence or destination to anyone. Though they did not understand, the girls obeyed. Soon thereafter, an annoyed Bimnono arrived with her fussy toddler Lusala and enough supplies for the trip. Isoke and Chimelu boarded the back, and covered themselves. Bimnono would travel under the guise of a Sanguë refugee returning to her homeland to bury her dead from the earthquake. No preparations were made for a return.

The lateness of the hour meant a quiet drive through Nozi, as the curfew for free travel for all had passed. Only those possessing legal documents from Kgosi himself were permitted to move this late. The seal Aitan placed over the fake documents was crude, but hopefully enough to pass for a legal wax mark by torchlight.

Bimnono's sweaty hands tightened on the leather reins, as the vehicle neared the heavily-guarded rear gates. Imposing figures, even in the dark, the guards might attack without reason or provocation. She stopped the cart, drawing Isoke's curiosity, though she would not uncover herself or her sleeping child to look. If it were trouble, they may jab at her with a spear. She positioned bags of grain around them to prevent this.

The men did not move – neither to check the cart, nor to open up the city gate. Bimnono propped Lusala up and left her vehicle, which, at another time, might have spelled her demise. The guards were unmoving statues. She approached them, slowly at first, then more deliberately. Still, there was no movement.

Giving into a latent desire, she slapped the guard's metal helmet just below the headstrap. The empty apparatus spun two full rotations before resting in its original position on its wooden beam for a head. Giggling, she opened the gate doors and ushered the cart through, past the snoring, unarmed men on the other side.

The next morning at breakfast time, Letsego burst in unannounced to claim one of Isoke's delicious bowls of cornmeal porridge. Instead, he discovered his younger brother raucously fumbling inside the kitchen. "You have about as much business in the kitchen as a swine in the temple. Why do you pester yourself with women's work?"

"Look around, brother," said Aitan, stirring the inside of the pot above the fire. Sakina and Madiha patiently waited for their bowls to be filled, but Bimnono and Isoke were absent. "Do you see a woman? My wives have been summoned."

"To the palace?" he asked, confused. "For what purpose?"

Aitan removed the pot and scraped its contents into two bowls. He then gave it to his daughters, who stared at the browned porridge with black flecks. Unsure of what to do, they said nothing until Aitan sent them away to their grandfather for food.

"Who knows?" Aitan replied. "He may take them into his service, or perhaps they have offended him?"

Letsego chuckled. "Bimnono's breasts fill with milk and she speaks her mind. Isoke is unclean most days, though I have heard the Otī care little for such inconveniences. Go to the palace. Inquire of their status, if he grants you an audience."

"I will do no such thing, brother, nor will you. Kgosi is not to be trifled with, and we have much work to do. My wives will be along in time."

Aitan's persistence in dropping the matter put Letsego on the defense. His brother did not care for Isoke, but he did. Letsego adored her tusk-shaped eyebrows, brown eyes round like kola nuts, and pointed nose. Otherwise plain-looking, Isoke's lips curved like a half-moon and her figure had thickened since they discovered her lying at the bottom of the empty waste pit. Because Isoke cared for his daughters and handled his domestic affairs, Aitan would not divorce her so that she could remarry another – especially since his older brother coveted her.

Kgosi had not summoned her, nor did he intend to make Aitan's wives concubines. Aitan concealed the true reason and, whatever it cost, Letsego determined to retrieve Isoke and claim her for himself.

# FOUR

## THE SECOND MONTH OF SUMMER, TWO YEARS AFTER THE ESCAPE, 2 A.B.

According to Aitan's only correspondence long ago, no Otī looked for either of his wives in Nozi, nor searched the surrounding territories. He explained to Letsego and their prying neighbors that after the earthquake, both were summoned to the palace to either become concubines, or executed for offenses against the throne.

Inside, Isoke wondered, after two years and a moon, if their husband ever intended to send for them. Not that Bimnono's family treated them unkindly. That was not why she wished to leave. They were kind enough, in their way. But the Sanguë lifestyle ran completely contrary to Isoke's beliefs. Beyond polytheistic worship, they customarily slept with one another in public. Drunkenness occurred at any time and street fights were commonplace. She held Chimelu and Lusala close whenever she disguised herself and left the brick hut, a rarity in itself.

Indeed, EL smiled upon them. Not one hostile Sanguë discovered their presence, for if they had, the Sanguë king would have heard of it and delivered them to Kgosi. Inciting trouble over minutiae was their way. And, thus far, Chimelu showed signs of normalcy – though Isoke watched him closely.

At suppertime one night, while Isoke and her son first gave thanks to EL at a separate table, Bimnono and Lusala ate freely. According to *Njia*, the quartet could not break bread together, as doing so would be communing with unbelievers. The Uché consumed only certain types of foods unblessed unto foreign gods. Often, this became a contentious issue for their hosts, as the adjustment resulted in added expense and efforts to conceal the harboring of runaways.

"So," said Bimnono, lips smacking. "Heard any word from Nozi?"

Isoke produced two sealed scrolls and smiled. "I was too nervous to open them myself. I thought we might read it after supper. It came this morning by messenger."

With no respect for protocol, Bimnono slid over to Isoke and grabbed the documents. "It is about time! You know it *must* be from Aitan," she said, excitedly. "Just look at the clumsiness of the forged seals. Who else but our husband?"

As the children ate, the two women read. Indeed, Aitan had called for them. Kgosi fought and lost a battle with poor health. His son, Kgosi II, who the Uché called "Muuaji," rose to power. The other scroll permitted them a travel allowance in case Otī confronted them. If the women departed before dawn, their arrival would coincide with the gathering of mourning crowds, drawing attention away from an oxen cart driven by a Sanguë woman. They would not need the additional permissions.

"Cool water to my thirsty soul! We can return!"

"My family would not let us stay another moon anyway. And Chimelu is approaching the. . ."

"I know," she interrupted, "that us being here is a burden to them. I am sorry."

"Yes, *you are*," Bimnono said. "But we are no longer welcome as well."

"Then, I suppose we have no choice?"

"No, we do not. You pray to your god and I will pray to ours for safe travels."

That night, Isoke lay on her back with Chimelu at her side. A small fissure in the roof leaked a beam of moonlight into the room. She stared directly into it and it gave her peace. Despite Bimnono's obnoxious snoring and that of her family in the adjacent room, she drifted off. She dreamed of returning to Nozi amid sunshine and rainbows, feasting and celebrations. No, Chimelu met no harm. In fact, he sat upon his mother's shoulders and smiled with glee, twirling colorful ribbons. His people celebrated him, for as he grew and matured, so increased their chances for freedom. Even Aitan smiled and held the little boy's hand.

The sensation of warm water droplets on her face interrupted her dreaming. She rubbed her eyes and let them adjust. Someone, or *something*, hovered over them. Isoke sprung up to defend Chimelu, but a cloth-covered hand silenced her screams before they could be heard. After being swept outside, he shoved her hard against the home's exterior and nestled a blade against her throat so closely that Isoke only managed slight whispers. Her own weapon, a sharpened piece of ivory with a crafted handle, was just beyond reach, strapped to her outer thigh. To stretch in any way would compromise its location – though she managed to graze its bottom with her fingertips. The hood of her attacker's cloak turned casually to his right, as if its wearer sensed something awry. The improvised dagger dropped to the ground at her feet. *It knew of Njia!*

Even in the moonlit dusk and faint light cast by the torch mounted into the ground, all she surmised about her assailant was the strength he used to hold her motionless. "What do you want?" she asked, though afraid of the answer.

She imagined a wicked smile beneath the cloak stretching across his face. His answer, a guttural growl, resembled an Uché name that she did not recognize. *Zarek.*

*I knew this day would come.* Without much room to move, she raised her knee as high as possible to where she imagined his crotch would be. This drew a laugh, but distracted him long enough for Isoke to grab the blade from between her toes and thrust it into his midsection. The assailant clutched the handle and fell to his knees.

Isoke removed it and tossed back the hood, revealing a bald, ashen face scarred by marks that were unmistakably Uché, but of the ancient language. The one mark she did understand was a branded number that lay above his right ear.

"Identify yourself!" she yelled with disregard to her surroundings.

"I am of the first. . .," he said, blood pooling in his mouth. ". . .not. . . the last."

Isoke rushed inside and hiked a still-sleeping Chimelu onto her shoulder. She searched the other rooms for intruders before returning to the main room where she slept. "Bimnono," she said, jabbing the blunt ivory into her former agitator's ribs hard enough to arouse her from sleep. "Get up! We have to leave. Now."

"Have you not the sense you were born with?" she slurred. "What difference does it make, now versus later? Evil spirits lurk in the darkness, seeking to devour those foolish enough to travel. Go back to sleep."

Isoke continued to hit her until her cracked eyelids revealed a panic-stricken houseguest holding a bloodied weapon in one hand and sleeping child in the other.

"What happened to you?" She pointed at the gore-stained blade. "Whose. . ."

". . .this *thing*. . .attacked me and carried me outside."

Bimnono pushed herself up and grabbed a weighty iron sword from beside the cooled hearth. "You cannot let evil lie! You have to cut off its head so it does not return." Upon reaching the attack site, she discovered no trace of blood or even distress marks in the ground. "Are you certain that you barricaded the door? You were the last one to come in."

"Yes!" Annoyed, Isoke surveyed the area for evidence. *Impossible!*

"It was probably just a street thief. It does not explain how he got inside, though, or the blood. Did he come through the window? How did he just *vanish*?"

Isoke feared the worst. *Can a master of dark arts*

*disappear?* "He said that there were *others*. He knew of
*Njia*. And he bore a mark at his ear that looked like this."
Isoke shifted Chimelu to her hip and drew a symbol in
the sand with her finger. "I think it is a number."

"Our language is derived from yours. It *is* a number. I
have seen it before."

"Where?"

"Mind your things first. We must leave before he
returns, or alerts his master."

Her avoidance of the subject did little to console Isoke,
who kept most of her and Chimelu's belongings packed
at all times. She quickly slipped on clothes and gathered
their remaining things, as Bimnono did the same and
bridled the oxen. They did so silently. Unless Bimnono
told her prior to leaving – which she did not – Isoke would
have to wait for an answer as to the number's
significance until they stopped.

The cart traveled faster in departure than it had in
approach a time ago. Even with the dawning sun at their
backs, the animals still saw just a foot in front of them
but knew the terrain well. The expiring of the third watch
presented a fortuitous time for those skulking along the
roads to attack unsuspecting travelers.

Bimnono kept a sword and steadied her hand on the
handle of one whenever the cart wobbled – often on the
rocky terrain. In the back, Isoke cradled Chimelu and
sang softly to occupy the time and, in part, to calm her
own nerves. While the cart was subject to attack from the
front, it also faced peril in the rear. With the driver
occupied, a robber may jump on and unload the cargo,
piece-by-piece. Lifting her would be a small feat, as she
did not weigh much more than she did before pregnancy.

At dawn, the group stopped along the banks of the
District River for a quick meal. Both Chimelu and Lusala
enjoyed the fresh air, sunshine and freedom to move
about. Bimnono gathered the fire, while Isoke prepared
cornmeal porridge with a sprinkle of cane sugar and
goat's milk. Thankfully, both Sanguë and Uché ate it, so

she separated the utensils. After separately blessing the food, the pair fed their children in virtual silence and allowed them to roam a short distance from where the oxen fed and drank.

"Eat in haste. The Otī frequent this region."

"If your EL is supposed to protect you, why do you worry so?"

"Easy for you to say," Isoke said, dousing her face clean with water from the banks. "No one pursues your head or Lusala's."

"So, let me ask you this then. . .out of all of the gods, even *Adui wa EL,* how do you know EL is the only *true god*? Perhaps another will protect us?"

"No. It is not so."

"And if you are *wrong*?"

"I have faith that I am not. But, I suppose. . .I live a good life and hope that whoever controls my soul will then have mercy on me."

"Will EL have mercy on those of us who do not believe in him?"

Isoke remembered an early teaching about EL casting unbelievers into a bloody, fiery abyss, but did not subscribe to the thought. "I do not know."

Bimnono smirked. "We are not so different, after all."

"No," she admitted, "I guess we are not."

"Your attacker said the name *Zarek*, did he not?"

Isoke's eyes lit with recognition.

"Do you know the story of Zarek, as according to our legends?"

"No." Sanguë believed in stories regarding *Njia* that the Uché dismissed –particularly about another branch of it that EL did not associate with.

"Zarek was the most favored herald of EL, so much so that EL considered him a son. There was nothing in the realm above that EL did not allow Zarek to do; raising the sun, sending the moon to chase him, and even controlling the seasons. Only one thing did he prohibit. His name must not be mentioned like EL's. No matter what he did, all adored and worshipped EL and did not mention the name of Zarek in praise.

"Long ago," she continued, "EL sent the very first holy rain, beginning this lower realm, along with humankind. This was the most magnificent of creations, and EL began to call *it* his sons and daughters. By this time, Zarek convinced a number of heralds to believe, as he came to believe, that EL would never allow him to be equal or superior. And because of that, the realm above should be controlled by Zarek and those he chose at his command. A war began. Though Zarek and his host fought, EL's heralds outnumbered and outpowered them, driving them beneath the earth in this realm. You know nothing of this?"

"No. If it existed as a text, it was probably destroyed."

Bimnono chuckled. "Stubborn Isoke, did your attacker exist?"

"What has one to do with the other?"

"The number of fallen heralds, threescore plus six, has been worshipped ever since then by those who consider themselves followers of Zarek. They cut it into their skin and became clerics of a different order, studying something called *Njia ya kifo*."

If her attacker was a eunuch, it explained the futility of her counterstrike to the crotch. "You are telling me that there are *threescore and six* looking to kill my son?"

Bimnono grabbed Isoke's hand and patted it. "What I am telling you is that there is a *legion* for each of Zarek's threescore and six. At the appointed time, according to the stories, Zarek will appoint a general and they will fight once again for control. They will do this by first destroying *Mkombozi* and then EL will be conquered."

Though prohibited against cursing EL, Isoke grew teary-eyed and looked into the skies. "You would grant my wish for a child and charge me to defend him against an *army*?" she yelled. "What sort of jest is this?"

Bimnono set a conciliatory arm about Isoke, which she rejected with fury. "Did you mean your seed to bring sorrow to us and not deliverance?" She shook her fists. "When we perish, your name will be mocked, along with those of the false gods!"

"Do not be so dramatic," Bimnono warned. "I do not believe in everything the same as you do, but you have to know if your EL is who you believe he is, then he would not send his son to rescue you and let him die before he can do it."

The rationale was logical, but did little to assuage Isoke. Suddenly aware that her son was out of sight, she called his name until he came running from a nearby wooded area, with Lusala in tow. Isoke clutched him tightly. His heartbeat against hers set Isoke at peace. *We will be fine, at least for now, and I need not worry.* They finished breakfast and boarded the cart uncovered, as they were now within good distance of Nozi and could travel somewhat freely. Besides, the oppressive midday heat might sicken a heavily-covered toddler.

The area did look busier and sound noisier than usual, and the work temporarily ceased for the funeral procession. Bimnono thought to continue on, but felt compelled to stop and investigate the commotion. Not soon after, those bearing the body of Kgosi drifted from the main thoroughfare. An audacious processional followed it. Horns blew fanfares in repetition until the crowd gathered in throngs. Bimnono hoisted Lusala onto her shoulders and jostled into better position to see the commotion. Isoke resisted the urge to stand in the cart and listened instead.

"Behold, Otī, Sanguë, and Uché alike, your king!" a courtier announced. At that, Muuaji dismounted his horse and kneeled just low enough to be crowned. After imbibing from a beverage Isoke assumed was alcoholic in nature, he accepted a bejeweled scepter and numerous gifts of tribute, including his father's seal ring. She wondered if Kgosi's body was still warm when these items were removed from it.

Without further delay – for the masses most likely

would bow before him, Isoke and Chimelu took off on foot. The distraction provided enough cover for them to escape. Strangely enough, when they arrived at Aitan's hut, none of her personal belongings remained. Pieces of the roof lay on the hut's dirt floor, with some angled into the chasm which, along with broken glass, almost claimed her husband's life. Pools of water collected at various spots and the air smelled of rotting flesh. Isoke hoisted Chimelu onto her shoulder, covering his mouth and nose with her hand. But he forced his way from her grasp and ran to Aitan's bedroom.

Failing to hesitate, she followed him, stopping short at the doorway and vomiting in the corner. He stood before a badly decomposed body. Vermin scurried across its maggot-infested graying limbs, while flies alighted on a large dark spot at the corpse's feet. She heard about the Otī treating Uché this way: torturing them unto death and forgoing even the indignity of tossing them away into the Valley of Bones by letting them perish in their own homes.

"Chimelu!"

In shock, he failed to respond.

Isoke moved closer, using her dress to filter the stench, and snatched him around the waist. *Little boys should not see such things.* Though she turned her back, Chimelu gained a full view of the body and reached out his hand.

"*Simama!*" he said. Isoke used that word often to summon Chimelu to his feet, and he repeated the things she often said.

Before they reached the door, Isoke heard a rustling. Then, a familiar voice called her name from behind. She caught a brief glimpse of a restored Aitan standing in the living area before slumping to the floor.

# FIVE

## THE SECOND MONTH OF SUMMER, THE AFTERNOON OF THE RETURN, 2 A.B.

An intense throbbing radiated from Isoke's temples. Eyes still closed, she squinted. Soon, a cool cloth covered her forehead. "Bimnono, where's Chimelu?"

"Someday, you are going to tell me how you do that. He is in the next room."

Isoke moistened her lips. "Do not think I that am crazed for telling you this, but I dreamed that Aitan had been killed, long dead, but Chimelu commanded him to rise and he *lived*. Mercy, I must have fainted from the heat."

"You did faint, but it was no dream."

She propped herself up on her elbows and looked around. "Aitan *lives*?"

"To the two of us, your boy, and the cleric alone, he lives. But hush! Letsego lurks about outside, as if we owed him burdensome debts."

Isoke's brow furrowed. "Letsego . . . Letsego," she sighed. "How I have not missed him. And the *cleric*? That crazed hermit who does not shave or wash, and eats bugs?"

Auni, who had prepared the damp cloth for Isoke, knelt at her side. "Do not mention Aitan by name outside these walls. If the Otī knew we had one who could raise the dead, there is no telling what they may do. He is in hiding."

"If what Bimnono says is true about Zarek, it may no longer matter. If you can count the specks of dirt underneath your sole, so may his chosen be counted."

Auni's weathered face darkened at the mention of Zarek's legions. *Indeed, he will be a formidable foe, if not*

– 49 –

*for Mkombozi.* "The boy must endure through the sacred rituals. Permit him to the temple with me. Another moon and he will be too old to initiate them."

Auni spoke of the boy's 777th day, by which he must be given over to EL, or else be rejected. Today was his 771st. Isoke hoped that six days would pass without ceremony and escape notice, but Bimnono had broached the subject during their return.

"You would instruct him to be like *you* . . . a recluse rejected by his own people?"

"It *must be*, Isoke. *Mkombozi* is to be the last cleric, not me."

"Where? *Where* is it written and sealed?" she interrupted. "Show me such a declaration and you shall have him this day. All you know is what you have been told, and retold to us for eras? Who is to say that it is even *true?*"

Briefly flustered, Auni almost appeared unsure of his words. "Speak softly."

"Your expression betrays you, cleric," she continued. "You *knew* of Zarek and his chosen, and did not mention his existence. What else do you hide?"

Auni backpedaled. *The Sanguë woman must have told her.* "Did you not witness Chimelu resurrect your husband from *death?* At least believe by that he is gifted in *Njia*, if all else falters, but my teachings will complete his total understanding of it. We do not even know that Zarek's legions exist."

"Whether they do or not, he will not undergo your rituals, nor become one of your kind. He will save us from Zarek, regardless of how the prophecies foretell it. *This*, I believe."

"And if he cannot, would you curse him and the rest of us? Should the blood of our young again run into the streets, their souls accusing you? What will you plead in defense. . .ignorance, indifference, or *insanity?*"

Isoke raised her hand to slap Auni when he accused her of being crazy, but she covered her mouth instead.

Without another word, the cleric exited Bimnono's home.

Isoke bent over. "Father, I do not know what has become of me," she whispered to EL. "I am not *cowardly*. Must I sacrifice my son and be *alone*? He is all I have. I am all he has!"

Bimnono handed her a cup of tepid kola to liven her mood. Isoke sipped from it absentmindedly. Condemning an entire race of people was never on the agenda, nor did she count on bearing the child of a deity and subsequently sentencing him to a life of solitude. *But if I do not give him over, will the blood of my people surely be upon my head?*

"I need to think." She lifted herself to stand. "Care for Chimelu until I return?"

"Be well and I will see you, if the sun so chooses to wake."

No sooner did the door shut before Letsego intercepted Isoke beside the doorpost, where he swallowed her in an embrace. "Dear sister, it has been two years and a moon! Where have you and Bimnono kept yourselves?"

"It was as Aitan said." She walked away and Letsego followed.

"It does not seem like the old king's way," he said, "for the Otī murder their harlots rather than release them. And do you not still suffer the blood?"

Reminded of her former condition, Isoke feigned appall. "Must you question underneath my clothes, Letsego? And when have you known the Otī to respect our customs? My only husband will be laid to rest in a valley and then be burned to ash!"

"No," he argued. "I have heard that Aitan is among the living."

Isoke said nothing to confirm or deny his beliefs, but stared straight ahead.

"I know how it sounds, but I believe it, as if I had seen him with my own eyes. Isoke, there are rumors of Uché informants passing information to the palace, and it has been told that a male child born around the last holy rain *lives*. If he is *Mkombozi*, knowledgeable in *Njia*, could he not snatch Aitan's soul back from the other realm?"

"*You* believe," she jeered, "that this boy survived the purges and is the *Promised One*? Nonsense."

Letsego smiled. "If he did live and the Otī discovered him, his parents would become enemies of the crown and their heads would decorate the new king's garden."

"Does all this posturing and discussion have a point, Letsego?"

"The existence of this child. . .we discovered one of our own betrayed Aitan unto death. Apparently, Aitan knew of the plot to hide the boy. They tortured him, Isoke."

She swallowed hard at the revelation, as it conjured up thoughts of the decaying corpse in the old hut. Despite his resurrection, Aitan suffered great pain and loss to protect her and the son he always wanted but did not sire. He revealed nothing, for if he had, the Otī would have found them hiding in the land of the Sanguë. "Many respected him well, and Lusala, Sakina and Madiha will miss him."

"*I* miss him and it stirs my anger that another would inflict this upon him. I overheard you speaking of a dream that someone named Chimelu commanded Aitan to rise and he lived again. Do you have Hawa's gift?"

"I do not," she truthfully admitted. "It is less a gift than a curse in my eyes."

"But if Aitan lives, and you know of it, tell me his location so that I may go to him and properly hide him."

Something about the timber of his voice set her on guard. "I tell you the truth Letsego. . .I have not seen Aitan since arriving to his hut."

"It is just as well," he replied. "This way, the Otī cannot look for him and his secrets can remain. But do not worry. I will provide for you now, as is our custom."

The pair stopped at a fork in the road. Isoke intended to continue to the temple. At this point, Letsego had to accompany her, continue elsewhere, or turn back. "Be well," he wished her, "and I will see you, if the sun so chooses to wake."

Isoke returned the greeting and then paused until Letsego vanished from sight. *He knows something. How much, I do not know.* Her whispers about Aitan were audible from the window. *Or did Letsego read my lips? It appears he solved the mystery of our two-year long disappearance, but it will not require much to poke holes in that theory. And if he investigates long enough, or persists in taking care of me as he supposes, Chimelu will be in constant danger of discovery.*

She erred back through the streets of Nozi toward Aitan's father's hut. There, she glimpsed through the window, long enough to see how the girls had grown during two years. Sakina, now ten years old, and Madiha, twelve, wore beautiful locks descending down their backs. The sadness on their faces were scars left by Isoke's and Aitan's disappearance.

En route to the temple, she cast her eyes in the direction of the flaming Valley of Bones. Only the Otī would set such a voluminous fire at the peak of summer with a wind blowing west into Nozi's airspace. This conflagration had lasted a full day and set forth its last few gasps of bright color flames and acrid smoke. Isoke tore her clothes and wept for her countrymen, as they had been denied their dignity of washing, perfuming, dressing and placement in a tomb.

Due to outnumbering the Otī by a large ratio and with no land allotments for burials, the Uché were forced to bury the dead in the Valley of Bones. Located at the edge of the eastern boundary and just south of the Great Mountain, the pit smelled of decomposition. When the scent became too overwhelming, the bodies were burned as an affront to EL, who forbade desecration to His most precious creation.

Therefore, each pyre required an atonement offering by the cleric. Isoke could have intercepted him in the outer courts while he prepared the sacrifice, but deferred. Tonight, she would enjoy the company of her infant son and deal with the repercussions later.

A week passed before something other than Chimelu's purported destiny and the increasing abridged rights of her people occupied Isoke's thoughts. Now, the Uché enjoyed no allowances for travel beyond the back and forth journeys to the marketplace. Muuaji hiked taxes so high that Uché children over the age of nine labored to supplement their household income, leaving no time for education. These things bothered Isoke enough for her to sneak small swills from Bimnono's wineskins to drown the swelling guilt.

At another time, EL would have struck Isoke dead for aborting his will. Though, in recent times, his anger cooled toward irreverence. In fact, he had not seemed upset much since the earthquake. In quiet times, she concentrated on the indiscriminate wave of leaves in the eastern wind and insects buzzing from flower to flower. She decided then and there that the land's beauty expressed love, whether or not the conditions of the heavens changed.

On the afternoon of the eighth day following her return, Isoke decided, after supper, that she would purchase a bird and slay it to curry favor with the deity, while also atoning for threatening Auni. Doing so meant an uncomfortable conversation, as he alone presided over sacrifices and shunned direct human contact. Isoke resolved to remain humble and handle her affairs quickly and quietly without fussing. *Perhaps I can escape the exchange without hearing about damning the entire race?*

She spied the cleric serving in the distance, as she assumed he would be. Composing herself, Isoke drew closer. His covered face indicated preparation for service inside the inner sanctum. It was the reason he immediately asked for Chimelu. Any later and it would be the beginning of harvest before he could be approached again.

Isoke held two bronze coins in her left palm, which he waved away. The cleric motioned for Isoke to follow him into the temple ruins. Only the area preceding the inner sanctum and the inner sanctum itself remained intact.

"What must you sacrifice for shedding blood in *murder*?"

"According to the prophets, for taking a life, another must be given equally in return," she said, bowing her head in reverence. "Blood for blood is why we sacrifice."

He turned his back. "Can a man give his life more than once for taking more than one life?"

Uché clerics routinely used lines of questioning as teaching tools. "Only if the dead rise. Then, he may do so, or as EL sees fit."

"You have spoken well, daughter." Satisfied, he removed his hood and turned around. "For you will see it happen."

"Aitan!" she exclaimed quietly and embraced him without further thought. Indeed, he wore solid flesh and bone and not the intangibility of a soul. "What do you mean by tricking me?"

"Do you not understand what must be done? Our people's lives depend on you. You once spoke to me of a belief that your son was *Mkombozi* and dared me to put you away or have you stoned, if you committed error. I have acquaintance with the fearful Isoke, who cowered in the presence of others and felt sorry for herself. But that day, you showed me the confidence of a trained soldier with his spear, which is why I sent you away and gave my life to protect you. Where is that conviction now? Gird up your courage once more and do what is required."

"He is all I have that is mine, Aitan. I will not leave him in the manner that Hawa forsook Fola and me. You could not possibly understand. You have another wife and three daughters. All I have is *him*. I am all he has."

His voice softened. "Because that is all you permit!

Only Madiha remembers Mairi, and vaguely. Sakina loves you, as if you birthed her yourself. Madiha does as well, and Lusala will learn in time. You are not alone. Neither will he be. You have not lost your mind, like your mother. You can visit him in the temple."

"It is not the same and he will not count Auni as kin. It is different for men. You gave your son away without remorse, which is something I would never do."

It marked the first time she had seen an emotional response in her husband besides anger. Aitan's face drew tightly, as if it had been knit together with threads of stone. "There is not a day that goes by that I do not think of Gamba. . .especially now."

"What changed?" she asked, incredulously. "You never spoke of him."

"Kgosi did come. . .for the two of you." He paused somberly, his voice cracking with regret. "One of my Uché brethren betrayed my trust. I do not know who."

"It may have been Letsego. I suspect he knows something about all of this."

"Letsego is fortunate to wear thongs on the correct foot most days. He would not turn spy for the Otī. I doubt he could do so competently. I told no one, especially him."

Isoke still pondered the possibility. "What has happened to you?"

"The things his guardsman did to me. . .I *died*, Isoke. I do not see things from your perspective, but then, you have not seen things through my eyes, either."

His tone struck a chord inside her. "What sort of *things*?" she prodded further. "You have seen EL's realm! What was it like. . .being in his presence? Everything we have been taught?"

"You know not of what you speak," he said tersely.

"And Mairi. . .did *Mairi* greet you? How did she look, magnificent in splendor?"

"Enough!" Aitan reassumed his former demeanor. "You have heard all you need to hear. Now decide, so the rest of us may live."

Isoke pursed her lips and stared Aitan down. "The Otī can come pry him from my lifeless body. Not you, not the cleric . . . none shall force me to give him up."

"Then those who seek him will find him, and when that occurs, they will do worse to him and doubly worse to you than that which was done to me. Turn him over to the cleric. It is the right thing to do to turn him into what he is destined to become."

She gave the matter some thought. He was inconsiderate, stingy and thought only of himself. Defending her and Chimelu did not bring him honor or financial gain, and he used to call *Njia* "a bunch of visual tricks, restrictive laws, and false hope."

"How do you know what he is destined to become?"

With his hand, Aitan tenderly brushed aside the hair at the front of Isoke's face and touched her forehead. "See for yourself."

Isoke's present reality shrank away, transporting her someplace so sweltering that she witnessed the transparent flow of heat waves. Sweat fell down her body as if a bottomless pitcher emptied above her head. The sensation of hot liquid sloshed and lapped vigorously about her feet. She did not need to identify it. Horrified by the smell of burning flesh, she coughed and retched. From her mouth sprung a wooden circle with four lines inside it that intersected a central line at two points. Isoke dropped the palm-sized object and marveled at her surroundings. She had heard of *Kuzimu*. Of the gods in their region, only EL condemned his doubters to a place like this: one of endless torment. *But why am I being shown? After all, I follow Njia! Those who endear themselves to EL are supposed to live forevermore with him!* If Aitan meant to inspire more doubt, he accomplished his task.

Isoke whipped her head to the rear, where the souls of her fallen countrymen beckoned her by name. She attempted to muffle the crying, the yelling, the screaming! The sounds echoed inside her consciousness. She slithered to her knees and wept miserably.

In the same manner which the vision appeared, it vanished. Isoke returned to the temple, still kneeling and weeping in front of her husband. The wretched symbol dangled from her fingers. Isoke dropped it and ran.

Auni descended down the steps and stood behind Aitan. "You showed her?"

He nodded, picking up the foreign object. "Everything, even this."

"Will she resist?"

"If her mind is set, she will die, even in error, to prove her point."

Isoke bounded from hut to hut, nosily peeking through open windows. By the fifth hut, several heads of households craned their necks to see the cause of the ruckus. One of them, a former commander of the Uché military named Fola, stopped Isoke from searching further.

"Where is she, brother?" she asked, breathlessly. "Where have you hidden her?"

"Calm down, Isoke. Who are you looking for?"

"You know good and well who I am looking for. Where is Hawa? She is not in the place of the elders! Do not bear false witness against me, or I swear, I. . ."

"She is *not well* anymore. She. . ."

"You allowed her to be sentenced to *that place*?"

"Isoke, she is not the woman you once knew. She is not . . ."

Before Fola could finish, Isoke fled for the western gate. Beyond it, close to a divot in the shape of the District River, is where she would find Hawa. Fola's emphasis on "not well" gave it away. The Uché referred to only one affliction in that manner. She discovered the place once before and refused to return to it after Mairi bit her own arm and cursed her best friend with a variation of every foul word in their language.

Unguarded, but surrounded by a sturdy wooden fence and beset on all sides by a modest tree grove, the hut gave birth to the most ungodly sounds, not unlike that of *Kuzimu*. For that reason alone, interpretation of what she had been shown, she would petition Hawa. If no one else told Isoke, she knew that the woman would tell her the truth without pretense – if she still bore her right mind.

# SIX

## THE SECOND MONTH OF SUMMER, THE EVENING OF THE RETURN, 2 A.B.

Isoke confirmed the sun's drifting western position. She would miss Nozi's curfew and pay a heavy price for doing so, if she did not hurry. Yet, as she weighed the consequences of her actions – standing before a sturdy, locked fence without a plan on how to get in or even back out – she cursed herself for being emotional and impulsive. Both the Otī and Uché cared nothing about the crazed and what they did for themselves or to themselves, as long as they stayed sequestered. Those who regained their faculties could find a way back to Nozi, or so the Uché assumed. No one committed to that place – at least to Isoke's knowledge – ever returned. Perhaps she would see Mairi, but did not wish to if her friend's condition had not improved. And the last time she and Hawa had met eye-to-eye was years ago, so she steeled herself against the possibility her own mother may not recognize her anymore.

In her adolescence, however, she wished not to be recognized. Not only did the constant flow of blood constantly drain her vitality, but it stripped Isoke of the ability to enjoy life and relationships outside of a sick hut. Hawa shuttled her to every physician in Nozi and, like Aitan did years later, spent considerable sums of money doing so. Still, no cure was found – which further angered Hawa. Only the incessant study of *Njia* and the proliferation of Hawa's foreknowledge gifts gave Isoke relief. They were also the catalyst for her mental instability. From the time that she abandoned them forward, Fola cared for his sister until a holy rain cured their father, but not their mother. Fola did so again following their father's death, but prior to her marriage.

After a long while, the hut's door opened, illuminating the immediate area and filling Isoke with hope. A crowd of men and women of differing ages spilled out into the weed-filled courtyard. Hawa stood in the midst of those acting more primal than civilized. Isoke followed the diminutive figure that made a beeline to the horizontal intersection of the wooden planks and busying itself by singing off-key. Isoke searched the woman's eyes for a hint of mental cogency, finding only vacant pupils. *Fola did warn me.* This Hawa did not resemble the same seer who predicted Chimelu's miraculous birth, nor the mother who raised two children close to adulthood. She, like other Uché seers unskilled in how to control their visions of the future through *Njia,* lost the connection to the present age and descended into insanity.

"Do you know who I am?" Isoke asked.

Hawa smirked. "Of course I do, daughter! Did you bring me something?"

"I did not bring you anything, Mama. I did not think that. . ."

"Your mother must not have taught you manners well."

Isoke's lip trembled. *My mistake.* Elders and seers called all young women "daughter."

"No. I suppose she did not. She was not around much. Pursuit of her beliefs held more importance to her than loving an ill daughter."

Hawa stroked the splintered contours of a plank, sighing. "Do not speak ill of your mother. Say, did you bring me something?"

Thinking quickly, Isoke yanked a violet flower from the ground and pushed it through the fence. "Yes, I brought you *this.*"

"So pretty! Thank you. Your mother must have taught you manners well. Will you tell me a story? I would love to hear a good story."

For a second, Isoke thought lucidity returned to the seer's mind, so she described the vision in detail from beginning to end. Hawa's head jostled playfully back and forth, as if she shook its meaning loose from her consciousness. Isoke finished, pausing in expectation of an interpretation. After receiving no response, Isoke banged her fists against the fence and looked off into the horizon. *The trip was useless! If I depart now, I may avoid a severe whipping for breaking the law.*

"Stay." Hawa grasped Isoke's wrist through the fence. "I get so very few visitors. Please stay a while."

In trying to free herself, Isoke noticed raised skin on the seer's palm. "Did you hurt yourself?" She examined it. It was the symbol from her vision! "What is *this*?"

"*The Revelation Gate*," Hawa said, matter-of-factly.

A weight dropped in Isoke's soul. "*That* is the Revelation Gate?"

"No." She shook her head. "It is much bigger. Big enough to fit a man's body."

*How does she know about the Revelation Gate? Why did she burn it into her skin?* Isoke squatted enough to see through the fence. "*Where* is the Revelation Gate?"

"My dear," Hawa said, caressing Isoke's cheek. "It is not for you to find; only for him to find, and those who usher him to it. Do not worry. You will see him enter it, but you will not watch him exit it."

Determined not to waste more time, Isoke resumed pursuit of the task at hand. "Will you interpret my vision, seer?"

"There was this sick little girl," she said. "The healers did all they could. She could never have children. She was unclean. . .a moon at a time. She suffered alone.

"She discovered a young bird had fallen from its nest. She did all she could. But she would not let it outside. She thought it would fly away and never come back to her. A short time later, it died. She cried because she missed it. The other birds looked for it, though it could no longer be found. They mourned it more than she ever could."

The story struck an aching spot in Isoke's heart. "I

understand," she admitted. "There is no power in this realm like a mother's love." She slowly withdrew from Hawa's grip, their fingers briefly intermingling. Hawa empathized with Isoke's pain and communicated so through reddened eyes. "I get so very few visitors. Please stay a while."

"*Stay?* No, I must be going. They will be looking for me."

Hawa laughed heartily. "They will be looking for *him,*" she corrected. "And if they destroy him, there is *no escape.* Then, you will see *Kuzimu* again, and when you blink, it shall not dissolve. This realm will belong to them. We will die forevermore."

She wanted to needle Hawa about personal matters, but all other questions fell short of being voiced. She would not answer them, nor understand. Isoke plucked another flower from the dirt and sent it through the fence. "Goodbye, Mama," she muttered. "Be well and I will see you, if the sun so chooses to wake."

"See you!" Hawa waved, with tears loitering beneath her eyes.

The punishment for missing curfew was a lashing. As soon as Isoke drew within sight of the Otī guarding the southern gate, they approached her with the intent to subdue. She surrendered and the sentries carried her inside Nozi. She undressed to the waist without protest, lay across the wooden post and adjusted her arms to be tied more readily.

She excavated pleasant old memories of the woman inside the asylum and draped them across the pain. She remembered celebrating the annual days of feasting, where eating and drinking delicacies seemed like excess more so than necessity. There, vintners introduced her father to the seductive nature of palm wine and Isoke grew affectionate toward kola. While the drink rendered the usual drinker hyperactive, it soothed her and lifted her mood instead. Isoke would invariably dip her hand into one bowl too many, or sip a little too much kola and end up with a stomachache. The admonition against gluttony followed. Curled next to the flickering hearth, for her condition rendered her cold even in the dead heat of summer, Isoke would listen to Hawa tell stories of Mosi and his legendary war battles. The boys thought Isoke strange to find interest in the tales, in some cases, more than they did.

Only a hard blow to an open wound snapped Isoke back to reality. The Otī guards had already untied her from the whipping post and yelled in their language to go home quickly, or they may beat her again.

She meandered about Nozi, stopping briefly at the window to Fola's home. She avoided catching the eye of his wife, who busily milled about the bedroom. She and Isoke loathed each other over the "unnaturally close" bond between brother and sister. Isoke waited until Fola looked up from his bed and locked eyes with him, long enough to communicate the bare essentials. *We had a conversation. I received what I sought. Mama is not well.*

Not long after Isoke gingerly removed her outer wrap once more did she notice cloths and a bowl of pungent liquid, presumably to clean the wounds. She eased down on the stool, again stripped to the waist, and started cleansing the lashing marks that she could reach – on her shoulders and the small of her back. Bimnono entered, just as the pain became too great for Isoke to continue alone. She wrung the cloth dry, dipped it and applied it to the separated skin bleeding the most profusely on Isoke's back.

"Whatever you did to receive this, I hope it was well worth the cost."

"What I did," she said, wincing, "is not as painful as what I am about to do."

"So, you have decided! Is it well within your soul?"
Isoke assented as much. "Is Chimelu asleep?"

"Yes. I fed him fish and bread, like you would have wanted. There is still some for you, or a little vegetable stew in the pot, if you would like it."

After everything, through their differences, Bimnono had become a friend. The thought nearly repulsed Isoke by instinct. Unwanted by the Uché and dismissed by the Otī – except for when it came to taxation – the Sanguë settled in seclusion on the southwest side of the wilderness. As intermarriage with them caused the occupation and captivity in the first place, no Uché wanted to willingly associate with them. It was one of the cultural barriers almost broken down by her former rival. Later, she may have a small taste of the stew and repent for it later.

Bimnono patted Isoke dry and dabbed salve on the wounds to cool the burning. *Tonight, it is impossible, but there could be no further delay. Tomorrow, Chimelu will begin training to become a cleric.*

The next morning, Isoke readily escorted her son to the temple, explaining on the way that what he did not comprehend now, he would come to understand at a later time. This seemed reasonable to the two-year-old, who said "yes," as if he knew he and the only parent he ever knew would be separated.

*But I am not abandoning you.*

Though a cleric renounced romantic and sexual involvement for life, other relational connections – like with that of a parent or sibling – were permitted in correct focus. Nothing must precede dedication to mastering *Njia*. She could not visit him every day, but intended to search for him on the day of worship, during feasts, and when she offered sacrifices – though she imagined Auni meant to keep him out of the public eye. Unlike his father Kgosi, Muuaji would not tolerate another cleric in the order, particularly one predestined to overthrow him. *Surely, the cleric will permit entrance to the mother of their promised savior!*

"I want you to know, no matter what it looks like, that you *are not* alone," Isoke said, barely holding her tears in check as she and Chimelu arrived at the temple ruins. "You may not see me daily, but every day, I am right here

. . .in your soul." She then pointed a finger at his heart and he erupted in a ticklish giggle. *"Always.* You are not a curse, nor are you cursed. You are my very special gift from EL. Do not forget that. And do not forget me. I will never forget you, or what you will do for your people someday."

"Mama!" Chimelu clutched her leg and asked to be picked up. Without hesitation, she complied, smothering her boy in a tight embrace and wet kisses until Auni interrupted. She handed him over to the unkempt cleric and pretended to ignore Chimelu screaming after her, as she turned her back and departed.

That evening, when Isoke's thoughts about him intermingled with her own feelings of abandonment and spun into complex webs of tangled emotions, she remembered the bird, and wondered how long Chimelu needed to spread his wings and soar across the open skies.

# SEVEN

## THE SECOND MONTH OF SUMMER, THREE DAYS AFTER THE RETURN, 2 A.B.

Unbeknownst to the general populace, the Otī nation – once great in its own eyes – stood at the tipping point of collapse. Muuaji had squashed the recent Uché guerilla revolts with heavy reprisals. But the events grew to be less of a nuisance and more a reminder that the captive race needed more drastic measures imposed upon it than curfews, travel restrictions, heavy taxation and population control through infanticide. Their spirits of resolve must be broken, and, following it, their collective will to fight back.

With Kgosi on the throne, the Uché relaxed and enjoyed its relative freedom – until he ordered the deaths of the young. For a night, footmen searched homes and, if a boy was found and esteemed to be the proper age, he was taken. Some defied orders, eliminating them and their families on the spot. By the time the wailing and cries sounded loudly throughout Nozi, it alerted the men of war ability, who defended their children capably until they were overcome. In the end, both sides lost too much that night to justify the means. By contrast, Muuaji would stop the bloodshed intelligently and not through heavy-handed taxes.

He destroyed EL's temple first, and outlawed *Njia* and its teachings – to little effect. For years, no one but the hermit Auni and a handful of worshippers even approached the place, and his men recovered no remains. *Has the fire burned long enough to consume the bones of my adversary?* If it had or had not, he no longer cared. Kabal, however, suspected the cleric lived after all. Either way, reducing the place of worship to rubble was a move of good faith to the respected Otī, who wished for the eyesore to be erased from existence long ago.

Following this, he set plans in motion to confiscate all coinage and valuable land from the Uché, redistribute it to only his people, who would then pay higher taxes than ever before. The subjugation would come about through forcing the Uché into manual labor – expanding the kingdom and its infrastructure from its current end, through the wilderness, to the southeast and beyond. Muuaji would employ Kabal to oversee the creation of the work force, thus, necessitating his replacement with one of his own whom he trusted.

Accomplishing these changes through force required all Otī men of ability to have military training. While the Sanguë would remain free, their men would *volunteer* to become part of the army and their able women to aid however necessary. Based on numbers alone, if the Otī stood toe-to-toe against the unarmed Uché, even in league with every Sanguë alive, they would lose.

The Otī needed an *advantage*.

Muuaji pondered these things at the window of the throne room while overlooking the vastness of his potential kingdom. As if on cue, a dark magician entered the king's presence unannounced. Startled, the king assumed a fighting position, as Kabal, his chief guardsman, announced visitors and not the visitors themselves.

"This is how you approach royalty, magician?"

"Quite the contrary. I have stood before kings before. Forgive me."

As he steadily rotated his magicians dependent on his pleasure or displeasure with them, Muuaji did not remember whether he had seen this one before. "Then, you know how to be escorted in and out! Kabal?" He had always questioned Kgosi's wits in appointing an Uché as his right hand. Now, the foreigner left him defenseless.

"Would you have me removed from your court before revealing the gods' will?" The magician, whose tone was blanched set against the king's rich, dark skin, bowed his head in obeisance. "You seek to expand your kingdom's strength."

"Yes," Muuaji hissed, still searching for his chief guardsman. "Kabal?"

"Others live up the District River, called *kusini mwa watu.*"

His eyes bulged. "You *dare* speak Uché in my presence?"

"There are no words in the Otī tongue to describe them, your majesty. They possess weapons that will grant you the unlimited strength you seek."

"How do you know these people exist?"

He bowed. "It is my business to know, sire."

"And what must I trade to gain this strength? Jewels? Currency?"

"*People.*"

The idea had never occurred to him before that moment. *By trading away some of the Uché, their numerical strength will weaken without castration, which causes higher rates of illness and death than I prefer.* "Tell me more, magician."

"Send spies west, past the land of the Sanguë and through the unexplored wilderness until you reach a cleared area. There, you will find them."

"And if they are savage, or do not speak?"

The magician chuckled. "Let your gifts do the talking."

Muuaji would do so, but it required more thought than just sending spies. The men must be heavily armed to defend themselves and bear the best of goods. "You have spoken well, prophet. I will send for you again. Name yourself."

"*Zarek, my lord,*" he said, ominously. "I will await your call."

Shortly thereafter, Muuaji retreated to his chambers, as Kgosi used to do before making weighty decisions, and called for Penda to relieve him. Still vibrant, she sashayed before him in brightly-colored robes. Her bone-straight hair dropped past her chin and she mesmerized Muuaji with the back-and-forth swishing of her hips.

Muuaji wasted no time, strongly embracing her and forcibly kissing Penda on the mouth and along the neck. Before she knew it, he had disrobed her and thrust himself upon her. Unlike his father, a deliberate, but selfish lover, Muuaji was about the quick conquest and the ends, not the means. Inside, she wondered if this poor treatment was payback for her dismissal of him while Kgosi lived.

Soon, he had finished and redressed, as Penda lay on her back to contemplate what had just happened. Next, would be the conversation. She wished he would bypass the illicit consorting and just talk so she could bathe and scrub off his scent.

"Your people are to be traded soon," he said, hoisting his pants, "and enslaved."

Penda sat up. *"Enslaved?"*

"Yes," he said in flippant fashion. "They will be traded for weapons and for whatever it is that I see fit. This is good in my estimation."

"I do not understand," she admitted, trying to mask her true feelings. *"Slavery?"*

"What is there to understand, Penda? They will construct grand buildings and monuments, clear my roads, and mine precious minerals and jewels for my pleasure! They will tear down my storehouses and build larger ones for excess! And, I will trade them for weapons and know-ledge that cannot be overcome. . .by might or power.

"My people will adore me for this, more than they do now. Your people, whether they survive or not, make little difference. The Sanguë will remain free, but as part of my enlarging empire." Pleased with himself, he chuckled heartily. "Indeed, this is *good!* Zarek has spoken well."

Penda clutched the sheets, biting her lip to hold back her tears. *Zarek!* "Well," she said with confidence. "You have judged wisely, my king. And what will happen to me and the other Uché in your court, I pray? What of my family?"

"You will continue in my service, as will Kabal and the others. Muuaji kissed her on the cheek and fondled beneath her chin. "You will continue doing what you do best. Your family, naturally, will be slaves. Should you leave this temple, you will become *worse* than them. Do you understand these things?"

"You have spoken well," her voice trembled to a whisper. "*Maafa.*"

"Disaster, indeed, of the worst kind!" he said, departing his chambers. "See your way to your quarters. And do not speak the Uché language in my presence again."

Only after she knew Muuaji was gone did she weep. *Slavery?* She thought of her parents and sister. She had not experienced a feeling of death inside her soul since living inside Nozi's limits. She tore her clothes in mourning and began praying, which she had not done with fervor in six years.

"Father, is it to be so? Are your people to be treated less than cattle, and your name to be ridiculed across the earth? Your people cry out to you, our blood seeps into the ground, and soldiers relieve themselves on the ashes of your temple!" She bowed facedown at the bedroom's large window. "Shall these cruel men who mock you persevere? Shall we finally be avenged at your hand? Or, shall we be slain forever?

"You saw fit to cure me of sickness, but not to rescue mine from certain death. I lack understanding, for you are EL, and your thoughts are mysterious to us. Now, I place a demand on you to redeem your words." Penda stood and pointed at the sky. "Your prophets spoke of *Mkombozi*, your son, and the Revelation Gate. If you shall strike me down for insolence, then do so! Claim my soul for your own. But if you should not, then send *Mkombozi* to deliver your people from this disaster that awaits us."

Penda dabbed beneath her eyes with a torn-off section of her robe and exited Muuaji's chambers, bumping into Kabal. The two exchanged glances. *Did he hear my pleas? If so, will he turn me in?*

He nodded for her to proceed. She did so without question.

Without knowledge of where he had been prior to a moment ago, Kabal considered how to describe his delirium to the king, who may have his head regardless. He did not give himself to palm wine, not since before dedicating himself to the study of *Njia. What happened?* He remembered nothing, besides encountering a magician in the passageway leading to the throne room. If he was to die, he wished to do so pleasurably. Officers of the royal court, even an Uché guardsman, could not be refused by an Otī harlot on the basis of race. After sleeping with her, and eating a meal of rich meats and delicacies, if Muuaji sought after him, Kabal determined to die with honor instead of running or hiding like a coward.

Hours after their first confluence, Muuaji summoned Zarek, who appeared in the main courts at his command. "Speak what you foresee, prophet."

"Gather twelve of your best, most fearless warriors, and send them to the edges of the wilderness. They must be led by an Uché."

"Kabal will not serve me in this capacity. He failed to appear before me when I summoned him. Such insolence shall only result in his head decorating my garden."

"Send him," Zarek admonished, "or your plans shall not succeed."

"You ask for too much, Zarek, but it shall be done as you say. If he fails, both his head and yours shall hang on poles."

"They shall take tribute – gold and fine linens, and a couple of Uché strongmen to demonstrate what you are proposing to offer them in exchange for militaristic resources."

The entire business sounded suspect to Muuaji, but he acted swiftly on the advice of his magician, pardoning

Kabal, and sending a group of eleven on the mission. In preparations, a day later, when Uché men traditionally left to work in the morning, Muuaji had three of their best, most physically-fit men bound, gagged and prepared for travel. The king ordered the envoy to return in no more than three weeks, to which Kabal gave his word.

The wilderness was indeed wild, as the group stopped numerous times to slay or deter vicious animals crossing their paths. As the Otī palate was indiscriminate, each night at camp, they ate the roasted carcasses of the beasts they deemed edible. They forced the Uché men to eat the same, which was deemed unclean by ceremonial law. If they spit out the food, Kabal whipped them and forced it into their mouths. The outlaw of *Njia* meant that even the faithful sometimes were forced to eat what the Otī ate.

The guardsmen rotated during the night to ensure that they would not be ambushed – either by *kusini mwa watu* mistaking them as foes meaning them harm, or the predators of the land. The estimated four-day journey actually stretched into seven due to constant stopping and the misjudged distance between the land of the Otī and their destination.

On the morning of the eighth day, the men secured their vehicles to makeshift stalls and approached on foot, quietly surveying the property of the *kusini mwa watu*. Unlike the clay huts of the Uché, Otī, and Sanguë, their homes were made from what looked to be the hardened foundation of the earth. The vehicles they used for travel looked similar to that of their eastern counterparts, but the yoked oxen were more handsome and sturdily built. The *kusini mwa watu* farmed well. The eyes of the Uché men widened, and they thought only three races existed. The prisoners were not permitted to see the land and could not understand the descriptive language of their captors.

Kabal instructed half of his men to stay put, and the

remainder to follow him with the slaves and tribute. Still a considerable distance away, Kabal and his men were halted at knifepoint, disarmed and escorted by armed *kusini mwa watu* to what the men assumed was the residence of their leader. The captives were unbound at the eyes and mouth, but not the hands or feet. Immediately, they started yelling, cursing and spitting on the Otī, which led to a gagging.

The building they were ushered into was larger than any structure they had ever seen, including Muuaji's palace. It was also composed of a rough, but harder-looking surface than their red clay and straw. While the escorts spoke to one another, Kabal backed against the wall and felt it. The Otī discovered this stony material beneath the earth's crust while digging for water, but never thought of excavating it and using it for structures. *The kusini mwa watu are advanced. What use will they have for slaves? We very well may have been sent on a fool's errand by our misdirected king.*

The Uché men studied the *kusini mwa watu*, in case they may ever get to describe them to their countrymen. Their facial features were not nearly as rich and round as the Otī, but less sharp than that of the Uché and Sanguë. In terms of physique, the men were a length or two taller than anyone Kabal had ever seen and were solidly built. Their unpolished language was rough and guttural, a bastardization of the Uché and Otī tongues. Kabal, the only one fluent in both, understood it only if they spoke slowly, so he could pick their sentences apart.

"Where did you find them?" asked the superior of the one who captured them.

"The west end. They bring tribute and these strange-looking ones as captives."

"Do you understand them, or they you?" The superior witnessed Kabal's eyes following their lips. "*He* understands. Take him inside and lead the others away!"

The officer obeyed, as his subordinates led took Kabal's men and the Uché to holding cells. This palace

put Muuaji's to shame. Precious metals decorated everything, from the throne itself to its surrounding obnoxious
accoutrements. The ruler who sat on the throne, a man
at least twice Muuaji's age, smiled at the approaching
duo. He did not seem at all surprised. The officer took a
knee and Kabal did the same out of reverence.

"Arise, brother," said the ruler. "I am *Kaizari Amiri
Jeshi Mkuu.* You are surprised by my presence, but am I
not surprised by yours. Your arrival was prophesied,
Kabal, and so, preparations have been made for you."

"Whom do you worship?" Kabal spoke in Uché, as less
words of this new language were in Otī. *How does this
stranger know my name?*

Kaizari processed the language slowly and responded
in kind. "He is called by many names, but we call him
*Adui wa EL.*"

Kabal asked many questions, to which Kaizari
responded by leading him to the library. An untold
number of papyrus scrolls littered the walls. He removed
one and spread it across a wooden table. The words were
written in an ancient dialect of Uché, which Kaizari and
his people wrote and spoke. While Kabal pieced together
parts of their speech enough to cull their meaning, he
could not make heads or tails of the writing.

"The oral Uché history has gaps," Kaizari said. "You
have been taught that Mosi was *your* first king. Here, it
speaks of *Adui wa EL* being the *first* king. He rules this
realm above me, even now. EL was jealous of him in the
other realm and banished him here. He and his heralds
consorted with mankind and produced us. Your people
call us *kusini mwa watu.*"

Kabal nodded, pretending to understand the text,
though only a few words were readable. "You are half-
human then?"

"Yes," Kaizari said proudly. "Threescore plus six of us.
From *Adui wa EL*'s bloodline and teachings, we are more
powerful in *Njia* than your clerics ever were, including the
eleven. We employ *Njia ya kifo,* as well, which your clerics

ignored for it is not passive. We understand its true power. They worship the wrong god. You feel this, as well, which is why you quit your clerical training."

"You know of my training?" Kabal was taken aback. *I knew Auni withheld something from me.*

"I know more than you can imagine."

Kaizari invited Kabal to the royal table for a meal. As they ate, Kaizari listened to Kabal explain Muuaji's offer – trading Uché men of fighting age to Kaizari in exchange for weapons and the expertise to create them. *But what advantage would mortal men provide immortal giants? There is something he is not telling me.*

Kaizari agreed. "We will infuse the Otī territory with our resources and you will provide us with the manpower to operate our infrastructure," he proposed. "Keep your inferior linens and meager portions of gold. Send me *people.* And tell your king I insist on only one other condition. . .that you and your descendants rule over the Uché."

Kabal grinned. *A king?* "He will never accept a regent in his own land!"

Kaizari waved to his cupbearer, who refilled the emperor's chalice with wine. "He has no other choice. War is brewing, in this realm and in the next. I will not trade my weapons unless this condition is met. And without them, his slaves will tread him underfoot."

"You have spoken well, my lord."

"Come then, King of the Uché!" Kaizari showed Kabal to his collection of concubines, more than five score at best estimate. "No king should be without a *bride.* Take the hand of any of them. I will not deny you."

Kaizari clapped grandly and the women lined up in rank and file. Kabal inspected the women top to bottom, front to back. He preferred the voluptuousness of the Sanguë and the color of the Otī. Only one fit the bill. Kabal inspected her like an animal would its prey.

"You have taken a liking to Sifa," Kaizari observed. "Take her. Enjoy her pleasures."

Kabal placed a firm hand at the small of Sifa's back. She bowed in humility and ducked out of line. Soon, the others recessed back to their quarters.

"Together, we will accomplish our destined future."

"What destined future is that?" asked Kabal, still eyeing Sifa.

"One of a new hope," Kaizari said. "You and your men have lodging. Go into your new bride. Stay with us a time and then be on your way."

Kabal acknowledged the emperor with a bow. Though he outranked him, Kaizari politely returned it out of courtesy. *A king! I will have my own palace, my own treasury! I will rule over the Uché and be free to ignore Muuaji's crazed notions. He will cede control to me, as I shall control a larger populace.* His revelry instantly consumed him. Only Sifa's gentle whisper in his ear alerted him to enter their assigned chamber.

Once there, he wasted little time indicating what his bride should do, though the formalities remained. There would be no exchange of property with her kin, for Sifa was the property of Kaizari, and the emperor granted her to him. Sifa's voluptuous figure and darker complexion suggested a background mixed with Sanguë, which disgusted him. When they made love, he treated her as such. At its conclusion, Sifa asked to be given leave to cleanse herself. Kabal allowed it. He watched his new bride exit the room, weeping in disgrace. Auni had taught him to shun the Sanguë; for what reason, he was not sure, except for their religion and something regarding "detestable practices."

What *was* detestable to Kabal was that, even though he volunteered to join the new clerical order, Auni insisted that he be castrated. He called his disciple "lustful and unrestrained." Kabal wanted things without knowing why he wanted them, other than someone else he admired possessing them. As a young boy below the age of accountability, he allowed his eyes to penetrate the clothing of his female peers. Castration had been outlawed by the clerics since the days of Mosi, but Auni said that he saw no other way to ensure Kabal's dedication to *Njia*.

That reason, along with the mystic contradictions of *Njia* – it could be used to defend and attack, rarely to kill – led to his defection from its path. He battled his master, and Auni soundly defeated him and cast him from the temple. The taste of that loss never fully dissipated from Kabal's consciousness. Kgosi forbade him to confront the cleric, for the former king feared *Njia* and Kabal's mortality. Muuaji had no such misgivings. The cleric's body had not been recovered from the temple's ashes. Auni still lived. Kabal knew it. He *felt* it. And, when he returned to the land of the Otī as king of the Uché, he would not be deterred in killing the cleric.

# EIGHT

## DURING SUMMER, ELEVEN DAYS AFTER THE SPIES ENTERED THE LAND, 2 A.B.

I n the tradition of his father, Muuaji lined several sharp, wooden pikes in the palace gardens to bear the heads of those unfortunate enough to cross him. At the area's rear, he reserved one for his chief guardsman upon his return.

The probability that twelve, highly-trained soldiers died in the wilderness or at the hands of a foreign people was low. *Insolence! Why else would they be tardy but for Kabal's lack of regard?*

Muuaji opted to hedge his bets on Zarek, but the magician mysteriously disappeared and could not be found. Now, without spiritual consult, or new weaponry, he was hesitant to proceed enslaving the aliens. *Tomorrow, I will venture to the undiscovered lands myself,* he thought. *Surely, they will not deny me personally!*

At the conclusion of his supper, which featured a dry portion of meat, the king and his cupbearer retired to the throne room. Shortly after issuing the command to impale the cook for preparing an inferior meal, Muuaji heard a battle call loud enough to draw alarm. He excused the cupbearer and unsheathed a short knife from his side. If the attackers endured the royal guard, he intended to fight it head-on. Metal clanged against metal in the distance, followed by a number of muffled thuds and crashes. Upstairs came the ruckus, past the guards posted at the throne room's entrance, with force terrible enough to make them scream.

The weighty iron in Muuaji's hand trembled. A secret passage of escape was blocked by his gold- and ivory-laden throne, which required four men to move. *The regular route will give my pursuers enough time to overtake me.*

Prior to the enemy entering the throne room, a small squadron and several magicians rushed to his defense. When the doors opened, one dressed as a king and nearly twice Muuaji's height led Kabal – also dressed in kingly attire – the eleven, and two other men of similar stature inside. While the two larger men wielded bloodstained weapons, Kabal and the Otī with him were not armed and did not look like they had struck a blow. *Had two men dispatched three score soldiers by themselves?*

"Kabal!" The king stepped forward from behind his squadron. "I send you away on a mission for this kingdom and *this* is how you return? What meaning of treachery is this? And why are you dressed in this manner? You look like a fool."

"You sent him to me in search of weapons," said Kaizari. "And I will set him as king over his people, the Uché, in exchange for those weapons."

"Under whose authority?"

"My master, *Adui wa EL*. Defy him at your own risk." Kabal translated the words into the Otī language, enraging Muuaji even more.

"I do not respect deities I do not worship. Leave my kingdom at once!"

"*You* did not have the authority to make me come," he said through Kabal, "nor do you have it to bid me leave."

Muuaji clapped his hands twice and his dark magicians reported front and center. "Then die."

At Muuaji's command, they tossed coarse powder in the face of Kaizari, who, along with his sentries, blew it in the opposite direction with mighty gusts of breath. The magicians and soldiers around Muuaji disintegrated before his eyes.

Disheartened, Muuaji raised his weapon with the intent to plunge it into his chest, but Kaizari transformed it into a harmless snake with a wave of the hand. At that, the king tossed his double-crown to the ground and knelt before Kaizari.

"A three-pronged attack is not easily defeated," he said through Kabal. "Arise."

"You leave me without honor," Muuaji said. "It is not possible."

Kaizari retrieved the discarded crown, the lower, larger, more ornate part representing the Otī kingdom, and the smaller, interlocking top crown for the Uché. He separated the two and placed the larger one upon Muuaji. "You shall retain control of the Otī and the Sanguë. Do with them as you please." He handed the smaller crown to Kabal, who donned it. "Kabal shall reign over the Uché."

Muuaji raised his chin. "Share my kingdom with *him?*"

"As it has been demonstrated," he snickered, "you have but little choice in the matter. *Adui wa EL* has foreseen it. An Uché king must rule again. You must continue to lord over the Otī and now, the Sanguë."

"I am a coward," he pouted, "and unfit to rule."

Kaizari gnashed his teeth. "You will rule because I command it! Arise!" Muuaji obeyed. "Enslave the Uché and trade the human chattel to me. Do so and I will arm you with weapons that will make you all but invincible. Use them to oppress your enemies and enlist the Sanguë in preparing armies for the conflicts that are to come."

Kaizari spoke so prophetically to Muuaji that he feared admonishing and would not inquire further. "Then let it be unto me, as you have said."

From there, the trio formally strategized until nightfall, as Otī servants prepared lodging for Kaizari and his soldiers. Flooding season was upon them and building another palace would be all but impossible in most desirable areas, except one. Kabal identified Nozi as the only consistently dry location suitable for its construction.

Razing Nozi also provided the land to be farmed out among the Otī. Landowners, thereby also slave owners, would assume higher taxes proportional to new land allotments and assessments. Muuaji licked his chops at the prospect of more money until Kaizari detailed the percentage he required for trade. He did not disclose what he planned to do with such an overabundance of currency.

But the displacement of more than three million people had to wait until harvest, which was two seasons away. Only Kaizari thought the delay best for all parties involved, for it meant Muuaji must sacrifice rooms in the palatial estate to accommodate Kabal and his bride, Sifa, for a longer time than either deemed pleasurable. Albeit temporarily, the once-allies now headed rival kingdoms and lived under the same roof as adversaries. Only Kabal focused on the possibility of the arrangement's disaster. Muuaji, too, considered the inconvenience, but spied Sifa's figure using the corners of his vision as a distraction.

Throughout the night into the next morning, the trio plotted the nuances of the slave system before installing it. Kaizari provided the tactical aspects, while Muuaji and Kabal anticipated potential problems. Gradually, Kaizari intended to siphon away a third of the Uché men of fighting age and select women of child-bearing age to his territory. By sapping the Uché of its strong men, Kaizari could expand his territory, and the women would provide pleasure to the slaves and possibly reproduce more *kusini mwa watu*. In exchange, he promised to send refined metal ore, wood and the knowledge to fashion armaments from them, the likes of which they had never seen.

To better control the remnant, according to Kaizari, Kabal had to sow dissent between the healthy, strong Uché men and women and the weaker specimens. First, as a message, he must do away with the sick and infirm in demonstrative fashion. Second, he should destroy the families, with the strongest and best men sent in to sleep with similarly suitable women. Lastly, by pitting the stronger against the weaker, the Uché would not band together against their common foes, but each other instead.

Almost six moons later, on the first morning of harvest, Otī soldiers awakened the Uché population and instructed them to remain inside. Some of the sturdily built men were shackled with irons and separated. Others were placed into a gated area between the Otī city and Nozi. The healthiest women were treated in a similar manner, sequestered beside the men, while their children were split and divided. Those who resisted were soundly beaten, bound and dragged into obedience.

Over the following few nights, the men were forced to construct crude living quarters from the materials they were permitted. As women traditionally tended the interior of the home and not its structure, they possessed no knowledge of how to construct these makeshift structures. Therefore, the men were expected to complete the task of building living spaces for everyone. This work was not particularly arduous, but time consuming. Besides, the anticipation of reuniting with their families helped pass the time and ease the labor.

Upon completion of the meager living areas, contrary to prior expectations, the men were set aside in one camp – those of fighting age and younger separated from those too old to war. The able-bodied women were divided by those of child-bearing age and those barren or those whose periods of uncleanness had ceased forever. The groups commenced harvesting – not for their race alone, as was their custom – but for the *entire country*. Several dozen of the thinner, but healthy Uché women, including Isoke, were sent to yet another camp and directed to function as wet nurses to the children that had not been weaned.

At that point, the most sickly and infirm, including those considered crazed, were invited to a special feast at the palace, courtesy of Muuaji. While some still observed the tenets of *Njia* and refused to eat with unbelievers, others did so fully and drank wine until their sensibilities slipped. From there, Muuaji escorted them to the royal garden, where Kabal and his men destroyed them all by the sword for sport.

Penda, who sneaked from her quarters along with a few of the other Uché concubines, and Sifa, witnessed the atrocity.

"Father, save us all," Penda said, turning from the window.

"Will you blaspheme the gods of your king," asked Sifa, "and be slaughtered alike? Forsake them and be concerned for your own safety. The walls have ears."

The two women slipped back into their living quarters unnoticed before the soldiers wantonly tossed the dead into a cattle cart and drove them a distance in close proximity to the new slave quarters. The sight drew many Uché, including Isoke, from their places of residence. They formed a crowd behind the fence, linked hands and wailed in mourning. The seers and elders were dead, the clerical order seemingly destroyed and *Mkombozi* still had not come.

Isoke wanted to cry and wail, like the others, but swallowed her despair and vomited unbridled anger. She could not protect Chimelu. His whereabouts had been unknown since the destruction of the temple. Madiha and Sakina had also vanished. So had Aitan. And Hawa's life had ended, too. The truth dropped into Isoke's soul like the wooden wheels of the cart. If she leapt into the pile of corpses and searched long enough, she would find Hawa's eyes still staring in judgment of her.

Isoke dropped free of her countrymen's hands and rumbled through the crowd, yanking the shoulders of several men before she found her brother.

"Fola!" she yelled, striking the man's midsection with open palms. Startled, he opened his eyes and nearly hit her.

Unafraid, Isoke stared him in the face. "Follow your instincts and strike me, Fola! Or would you fight those who would slay your elders like *animals*?"

Fola dropped his hands. "This is not the time, nor the place."

"When is the time, *coward?* Look around you. They herd us like cattle and will force us to dirty our fingernails with servitude until we fall face down in the dust. Then, they will deny us proper burial and toss us into a ditch! How long will we pray to EL, who refuses to hear our cries? I have lost *everything* . . . my son, my husband, my daughters, my *life!* We all have. Our mother lies in that cart, do you not feel it? There is nothing left! If I am to live as one dead, to mourn and grieve for the rest of my days, then so be it. I *will* die but I will not do it alone! They will join me."

Isoke's ranting had drawn a crowd of sympathizers, including Letsego, who inserted himself into the center of the commotion. Fola scanned the crowd. Around them, hatred flickered wildly in their reddened eyes. "Enough Isoke!" he said.

"Perhaps she has spoken well," yelled Letsego. "We should take up arms!"

"The spilt blood of our sons cries out from the mountains and the river's bottom." She pointed to the Valley of Bones. "Our elders, seers, mothers and fathers will burn in the distance. Are you all *eunuchs?* Be men and fight, or the honor of destroying the Otī will fall at another! Stop waiting, praying, and wishing to be sent a deliverer and become what it is that you seek!"

Isoke's passion whipped the crowd into a frenzied mob, but the Otī tending to the fledgling fire in the Valley of Bones interpreted it as mourning and smirked at the rowdy slaves shaking the wooden and metal fence poles.

It was then decided to birth an underground militia, with Fola as its reluctant leader and Letsego, who enthusiastically volunteered as its chief messenger.

# PART TWO

# NINE

## DURING SUMMER, 17 YEARS INTO ENSLAVEMENT, 20 A.B.

**❝** Make your mark!"

Isoke sharpened the broad head with an iron shard. Done correctly, the jagged prongs would tear out an opponent's flesh should he attempt to remove it. If the shape was off, the arrow would sail errant when fired, and each error earned her punishment. Isoke purposely marked it wrong and dropped it into the waste trough, drawing a stiff reed to her hand for wasting another precious import.

The overseer tired of her, as the bald slave frequently daydreamed and ruined too many arrowheads. Displeasure with a slave brought the whip, and when lashed, Isoke muttered nothing. The striking commenced longer and she still made no reply. She believed that the blows toughened her for conflict, though for twelve years now, the Uché mobilized and organized, only to postpone. The swords, shields and armor of a light brownish metal, and reed arrows Isoke helped construct gave the enemy a decided advantage.

As she whittled, Isoke wondered how much Uché blood this particular weapon garnered in trade. Considered too delicate to work the fields but of good enough use not to kill, Isoke and other women like her were put to work fashioning weapons or doing light housework. She no longer had to feign sickness, as the Otī forced those with diseases to mingle in the general population. Stronger women farmed along with the older teenagers, and smaller children helped. The men of fighting age and the strongest ones shaped bricks from mud and straw and constructed whatever it was that

Kabal decided he needed at the moment – even after the building of his estate.

Muuaji now exported Uché as a matter of practice, publicly beating and shipping the families of his servants to unknown portions of the realm. Isoke doubted that the arrogant king imagined the beaten-down Uché could muster a decent fight, and they could not. Their force had no single leader, but a collection of self-appointed generals who argued their points to tiresome lengths. Even Fola, who once held a position of esteem among the soldiers, had lost his voice with them.

"You wear my patience, *slave.*" The overseer snatched Isoke from her thoughts by yanking the hoop from her nostril. "This metal is *expensive*. Lose concentration again and see if I do not have you flogged half to death. Then, you will scream for me."

While a trail of blood fell down her face, Isoke defiantly bowed her head, plucked another iron from the container and continued her work. When the Otī's backs were turned, she would empty the shavings and waste trough, no matter how full or empty it was. In doing so, she separated the true mistakes from the intentional ones – arrowheads marked with a subtle cut on its ridge – and place them in a belt she had concealed under her robe. The overseers suspected nothing, for slave's robes were sewn from thick sackcloth, unlike the lighter dress of her superiors, and her indiscretions hid well. Had she not retained her natural coolness after her healing, Isoke would have long since passed out from the sweltering heat.

By mid-morning, she increased her efforts and matched one of her arrowheads for every three of the enemy. This earned the praise of her overseer and a five-minute break for a little nourishment. As Sanguë were redeemed from forced labor, Bimnono volunteered to work so that she could watch Isoke. She used the break as an opportunity to sidle up to her former rival.

"It has been some time now," she said under her

breath, "nearly 16 years. Where is your dignity? How long must you mourn the dead?"

Isoke spoke between bites of bread. "Your daughter lives. We celebrate what we have."

"You want Lusala? Have her," she joked.

She looked around at the unsuspecting faces of her oppressors. *How they will pay someday!*

"You once spoke to me about faith in EL and that trusting in *Njia* requires you to stand strong in the darkest of times. Where is it that faith now?"

Isoke knocked back the contents of a pitcher and let its overflow pour over her dry face. "My faith lies in the ashes of the temple with my son. Mind your own house and their soldiers may not relieve themselves on your child's smoldering remains."

"You people are all the same. When times are high, you are perfect, but at your lowest, look at you! Your people call us Sanguë 'dogs,' but dogs can enjoy themselves when they are down. There is no sorrow a drink or a bedfellow cannot cure."

Isoke rose and set the empty pitcher in Bimnono's lap. "Continue soothing yourself in ignorance, for it affords you little else. Drunkenness and licentious behavior does not cure sorrow . . .they *multiply it.*"

"Fine," she sharply replied. "Dry up like a bitter root for all I care."

Bimnono waddled away, cursing under her breath. When Isoke returned to her work, she pondered what the foreigner had said. From Chimelu's disappearance forward, only the prospect of impending war and revenge kept her alive.

A splinter group of the rebellion, of which Isoke joined, believed guerilla warfare to be noble in intent but misguided in effort – barely chipping away at the mighty foe. Since being enslaved, its members had covertly assembled arms from under the noses of their oppressors. At the appropriate time, and not before, they would assemble, cut off the trade routes, attack the Otī and Sanguë armies, and fulfill its main objective – assassinate Muuaji and Kabal, throwing the government into flux.

But even the most optimistic of Uché knew that *they needed a miracle.*

That first moon in the wilderness long ago prepared Auni for survival better than any instruction. For one, the plants forbidden by Uché law were either hallucinogenic or useless for food and the unclean animals were worm-infested and bathed in filth. Each of these – within reason – he tried, as circumstances demanded, and found them to be detestable. Whatever he tasted and thought good soured his stomach, which had been trained to crave certain things. Without those luxuries, he subsisted on wild fruits, the least muddy waters to drink and whatever vegetables he could forage.

His company, however, was a different story. To supplement Chimelu's diet, Auni employed the use of a goat that had lost itself among the woods. *EL be praised,* he thought, for the animal was well-fed, female, had just given birth and been lactating for some time. He milked the goat and, after boiling the express and letting it cool, served it to his hungry charge. In a similar manner, Auni instructed him in *Njia* from memory, for when he was forced to leave Nozi, an opportunity to retrieve the remaining texts did not present itself.

First, Auni drilled the unbreakable, sacred pillar of belief into him at a young age: *all things are possible to him who believes.* All else ebbed and flowed from that key element. Most believers, even the clerics, never moved beyond esoteric comprehension of the concept onto maturity. But he knew that the boy must reach true mastery in order to fulfill his ordained destiny as the Son of Mosi. The prophecies had foretold it.

While *Mkombozi* was assumed to be invulnerable, the text's original translation, Auni remembered, mentioned that the boy could be *mortally wounded* under certain circumstances – which circumstances, he was not sure. If Chimelu had any mental control over his vulnerability, doing so at a young age would be impossible. *Exactly why*, Auni reasoned, *a close eye must be kept on him.*

As the precocious youngster lived, his unnatural abilities slowly manifested consciously – the first surfacing their third season in exile, while Auni gathered kindling for a supper fire.

"Father!" A small hand tugged at his leg. "Look!"

Five years old, Chimelu presented a bug in the palm of his hand. The creature sunk its fangs into the child's tender flesh. He flung it to the ground and Auni stepped on it.

"You hurt him, Father."

The cleric examined the little boy's hand; it reddened and swelled just above a lump of rising skin. Doubt had entered his mind. "It harmed you. You are under my care. I am to protect you."

Chimelu bent down and touched the insect's crushed body. Immediately, its skeleton, blood and innards restored themselves and it flew away.

Amazed, Auni knelt to the little boy's height level. "Why did you do that?"

"I *forgave* him," he responded, matter-of-factly.

"Chimelu, you *must* be aware of things that can hurt you."

"Why?"

At that time, Auni had been looking for occurrences such as this, where his innocent charge would do something extraordinary. To this point, absent the bug healing and him raising Aitan from the dead, there had been nothing to report. The quicker the boy gained control over his abilities to effectively hide them, the better. Sooner or later, they may be found out, and without restraining himself, he could easily be identified. "It can return and hurt you again." Auni adjusted the frustration in his tone. "Whenever you *help* someone, you must not be seen. There are people out there who want to harm you."

"Yes." The boy hopped alongside his father figure in a nearby grass field.

The more intense instruction started with Chimelu's developmental marker. The boy understood how to heal and resurrect from the dead first; naturally, since he lifted Aitan at a young age. Next, he learned how to move objects mentally, though he struggled to control it. Much later, through much meditation and concentration, he mastered the abilities to alter the balances of chance and reality and to change the constitution of liquids and solids. This power brought Auni joy, as he despised the waiting process necessary to produce viable drinks other than water. This skill officially meant that the student had surpassed the master, as Auni did not possess it. He wondered what other things the boy could do.

Now, nearly 16 years after they escaped the temple under the cloak of darkness, he and the teenager waited for the flame to consume the animal they had sacrificed. For on this day, what remained belonged to them as food. Chimelu licked his lips, hoping EL may leave the thigh and leg portion, as those were his favorites – while Auni did not particularly discriminate.

"Why do we sacrifice?" Auni routinely questioned his charge, in part to test his memory and comprehension, and to gauge his growing powers.

"We do so when EL is displeased," Chimelu responded, "or when we have shed blood. We sacrifice to curry EL's favor, and in celebration of him."

"You have answered well, my son." Now 70 years old, Auni no longer moved as fluidly as he had in his youth. The past few years had taken their toll. Chronic pain seeped into his aged joints and his speech often slurred.

With only residual heat remaining on the altar, Chimelu readied his fork to tear into the leg at the charred hip joint, but the look on Auni's face gave him pause. "I hunger. Must we wait, although EL chooses his lot?"

"Show me your progress first."

Chimelu leaned his fork against the altar. He cleared his mind of occupying thoughts and sensations – the oppressive heat coaxed sweat from underneath his armpits, the center of his chest and his back. He shut out the sounds of wings flapping. Predatory birds lingered in the area should they neglect the corpse.

"Stop thinking about food and concentrate!"

Chimelu cracked an eyelid in Auni's direction. His teacher relentlessly paced and gesticulated with his hands. "If you are distracted, the Enemy has already won. Keep your eyes fixed on what matters, not me or the thigh and leg portion."

His mind finally clear, he opened his eyes to the altar which took him and Auni an hour to construct. They had rolled the heavy stones into place, one for each of the eleven martyred clerics who now resided in the other realm with EL, and a twelfth for *Mkombozi*, the final cleric. The slain sacrifice still lay on its side, consumed to the bone in all but two places – the left leg and thigh, and one whole arm. He focused on the pyre's platform first, keeping it level while he rolled away each stone away one-by-one. After the last stone joined the collection, he rearranged the usable wood to form a flat table of sorts and laid the animal down. Auni clapped his hands in mock praise.

"*Progress!*" he scoffed. "No washing off our supper this time."

Chimelu was not amused. On several occasions, his wandering attention dropped their food into the dirt. "Thank you, Father. May we eat now?"

"I have another test for you. Before *you* eat, move that, as well."

Auni pointed to a boulder 40 times as large as the others. *It is large enough to be the cornerstone of a building*, Chimelu imagined, *that might reach into the heavens.* "*That?* A moon may pass sooner than I budge it."

"Then, I suppose you had better start. Perhaps, I will take a nap. Rouse me when you finish. I suppose I could sleep a moon, if I determined so."

Auni served himself to the animal's arm and settled beneath the nearest tree to watch his adopted son attempt the task. Unlike previous challenges, Chimelu did not attempt it through physical force, for following *Njia* did not involve bodily might or strength. He rounded the massive rock, studying its voluminous shape and design, while feeling its composition and rough texture. Finally, he knelt in the direction of the sun and said something aloud that Auni did not hear. At that point, Auni shut his eyes in meditation and fell asleep. *Chimelu will wake me.*

The cooling breeze of the evening awoke Auni instead. Chimelu lay next to him, the bare thigh and leg bones at his feet. He thought he may have to discipline the boy until he saw the rock he told him to move – if it were to be believed. Not only had Chimelu moved it, but he had also smashed it into *grains.*

Using his walking staff, Auni poked Chimelu gently in the ribs; nothing short of blunt force awakened him. He stirred and flashed a winsome smile, knowing that he had done well and that his surrogate father would be pleased – even if he would not admit it.

"*Simama.* The time is coming when no man can work."

"Yes, Father."

The two trudged back to the modest accommodations that they had constructed in the wilderness, far enough into the woods to avoid detection. They used torches sparingly and kept inside during high times of travel for the Otī and Sanguë, and relocated whenever Auni perceived a threat of being captured – which was often. During recent years, he anticipated problems more than the usual, meaning that some days they ate and drank whatever they could. This was the hermetic existence of a cleric and Chimelu found much wrong with it.

He desired interaction with others his age. Auni was old and did little physical activity on most days, none on others. He lectured Chimelu in those times about *Njia*, his purpose and maximizing his life. It was valuable wisdom, but poorly packaged in rambling diatribes.

Chimelu wondered what his countrymen were like, as he had little memory of living in Nozi, a family, or the opposite sex. Nor would the cleric tell him. Forming attachments to the unknown could lead him to stray from his teachings and emotionally attach to relationships he could not nourish, more so than he did now.

Once, several seasons ago, Chimelu awakened confused by a sudden change in his body. Auni explained it away, saying that it was a typical experience of most young men in the morning. Then, he diagrammed the mechanics of procreation to Chimelu, so that he may avoid further thoughts of it. This deterred Chimelu, for as he knew so very little about interaction with human beings, his curiosity proved more tempting than anything else. Even worse, though he would become a cleric, he need not become a eunuch, like Auni. *I must master and control these new feelings.*

That night, as he lay on his mat, he pictured what *girls* must be like. He thought of his unshaven head and imagined theirs to be like it; long-haired, but in a different fashion. *They smell like blooming flowers, or the scent of approaching rain*, he thought. *Their voices must be different, higher, or softer.* He doubted that they produced sweat, moved their bowels, or used foul language. If he ever met one, he would touch her just to perceive the differences between his and her skin. Whatever she spoke of would captivate him for hours, he was sure of it.

Chimelu rolled onto his stomach and wondered about the limitations of his powers. So far, he discovered the ability to heal the broken or dead, turn muddy waters potable, and to manipulate the movement of objects, small or large, with his mind. Though he tried, he could not likewise propel himself or Auni. When asked about it, the cleric replied cryptically. "Who can lift himself up from the earth, except others lift him?"

While he *could* heal, Chimelu did not *always* heal. The plights of some wounded animals he encountered pricked at his heart and he mended those. Others he allowed to die and be plucked to the bone by its predators. He wished to heal them all, but discovered wisdom in selection. If some died in folly and were raised, they would die again in folly. Using *Njia*, according to fiery emotions like compassion, sympathy, love, or anger and hate was dangerous. What may be deemed harmless by the user often incurred a consequence that was unforeseen.

# TEN

## NEAR THE END OF FLOOD SEASON, 17 YEARS INTO ENSLAVEMENT, 20 A.B.

Shortly before the enslavement, with Aitan assumed dead, Bimnono fell in with an older Sanguë man. Too old to battle, but not to lecture, he gave his opinion to anyone unfortunate enough to be within earshot. He adored Bimnono's pear-shaped figure and the sassiness that his late wife never had the gall to give him. The couple wed and lived in virtual harmony; she ignored him, while he placated her. And Lusala learned to respect him, though she paid him no mind when Bimnono gave conflicting orders.

He did come in handy, though, when it came to suggesting Lusala's suitor, as the Sanguë retained individual rights and could still marry. Too cheap to provide her a decent dowry, he denied the father of each and every boy that came to the door, no matter how exorbitant the bride price was or how meager the dowry they would accept. As long as she lived underneath his roof, Bimnono's husband was resolute in making sure that Lusala did not participate in the lascivious activities of the Sanguë. It violated his traditionalist beliefs and Bimnono agreed. Too many girls Lusala's age suffered poor societal standing because of promiscuity, though the Sanguë did all but promote it.

Thinking that she may be dead and gone before she received what she truly wanted, the 19-year-old Lusala snuck around the Sanguë settlement with boys willing to experiment. At first, she just kissed them. Then, an aggressive one eased his hand onto her breast. She slapped him for it. The next one to try it walked funny for a day. The third did so in a sly, seductive manner and she permitted it.

This carrying on continued until Bimnono caught her daughter with her dress up. Though still a maiden, Lusala's reputation was growing. Bimnono explained with her balled-up fists why this behavior needed to stop; that no man would marry a whore. *Fine with me*, Lusala thought. *Who wants one of them as a husband?* She had a tough time quelling the fire, even considering the alternative that her peers advised.

So, Bimnono ordered her husband to find a suitable older man for their daughter and do it by the five days of feasting – giving him all of harvest and summer to do it. Lusala determined to get out of it, though she was unsure of exactly *how* to do it and marry the one she *did want*.

Isoke, on the other hand, fought Letsego at every turn since Aitan's disappearance. With the disbanding of the sick hut, she had to bear false shame in front of him. While her former condition disgusted every Uché man she ever knew, he seemed unbothered and *intrigued*. By Uché law, she did belong to him, but Otī laws prevailed. They outlawed marriage between slaves and she had not been paired for mating based on her physicality. It was an arrangement Letsego interpreted as an invitation to continue pursuit. If nothing else, he wanted to sleep with her. She said no and repeated it, until one day he tired of asking and forced the issue behind a hut. Isoke bit and clawed herself free and mentioned of it to Fola, who stayed in Letsego's hut from then on.

Whenever Kabal appeared in Muuaji's court, Muuaji addressed him with respect. But if Muuaji came to Kabal's smaller palace, he called him his proper name, Kgosi II. The latter interpreted it as a move of disrespect, but the former did not care. Both of them were equal; figurehead regents of territory under Kaizari's rule. Though Kaizari did not treat them as subordinates, they cowered at his ability to destroy them at any time. On this particular day, Kabal appeared before Muuaji prepared for battle, which confused the Otī and Sanguë king. The time for warring had passed and no foreign enemies presented themselves at this time.

"Some of my men discovered a small hut deep in the wilderness," Kabal explained, "so one stayed behind at a distance. Two Uché live there."

"Runaways brazen enough to build lodging? Who would do such a thing?"

"Auni," Kabal said, with disdain. "I believe I have found him. . .and his disciple."

"You have searched throughout the wilderness for years and found nothing but smothered fires. You search in vain. How many have you sent into the wilderness and lost to predators? Go back to your palace. Sleep with Sifa, or take a concubine, drink wine and feast. The cleric did not survive the temple's razing, nor does he train another."

"It *is* possible," Kabal insisted, "and if I find him alive, he will not live long."

Muuaji rose. A runaway slave would be Kabal's concern, but the destruction of the temple and supposed assassination of the cleric occurred under his watch; a failure that infuriated him. "I will send a squadron with you. Tarry until tomorrow. I will contact the spy I have planted in the Uché camp and verify."

"Do not bother. Auni is old and weak. My best men will accompany me."

"You will entrust me to watch your kingdom in your absence?"

Kabal laughed. "Sifa's son is too young to assume the throne. I have no other choice. My only consolation is that it will only be for a short time."

"Be further eased. I will protect them. I have run these kingdoms before."

"Yes," said Kabal, as he took leave, "but at that time, you did not have four million people wanting to kill you because you enslaved them. I shall return."

"Is it time to eat?" Dust-ridden, Chimelu burst through the door.

"Almost," Auni smirked, still preparing the meal. "But anyone wishing to feast at this table in this hut must not bring an accompanying odor with him as company or dirt cakes for a dessert."

Chimelu disappeared to his customary spot a minute's walk from the hut's east wall, where a shallow tub of warm water awaited him. He stripped down, jumped in and took care of business. Meanwhile, Auni tossed the meat and vegetables into a pot hanging over the stone hearth. By the time his ward finished bathing and had spent a few minutes more to play, the meal would be finished.

"Young one," said Auni, as he sensed the door opening, "I know you did not finish that quickly."

"Quite true. To whom do you speak, old man – an apprentice, perhaps?"

The baritone voice struck him as familiar. He faced the doorway. In it stood Kabal, outfitted in modest armor, a fierce blade hanging at his right side. The garrison's steely-eyed glare made the command "Freeze" clear without a word uttered.

He ignored the question. "You look prepared to destroy a heathen nation and not a crippled old man." His eyes caught his walking stick in the corner. Other than a blunted culinary knife at the edge of the cutting board, nothing else in the domicile resembled a weapon. Though his hands were gripped with severe stiffness, Auni could still clutch things tightly once his joints locked.

"You are hardly harmless. I have not forgotten *Njia* . . . and neither have you."

Auni sidled toward the corner. "Because underneath the evil, Kabili, you are still Uché."

"'Kabili,' and his pacifist manners are dead. You shall join them."

"Kill me? *Why?* Your coward of a master desires my head as a trophy, yet sends you for the task? He is a coward, just like his father before him."

"*I* am king of the Uché. . .my own master," he said in anger. Kabal reached behind his back for a sheathed dagger that Auni's dimmed abilities failed to sense. "It appears my premonitions of your survival were true, but presumptuous. . .assuming you would stay that way."

Auni reached out his hand and summoned the stick, commanding its center to a careful position at the meat of his palm. It obeyed, floating across the room in time enough for him to knock the thrown dagger aside onto the floor.

Suddenly, as quickly as it had been thrown, the blade returned handle first into Kabal's possession. Auni called his knife to his free hand's fingers and tossed it at Kabal, who dodged it and hurled his dagger again in one motion. Too fast for Auni to block, it plunged into his left shoulder underneath the bone and inches from his heart. Crimson dripped from the wound down onto his white robe. He dropped his pole to remove it slowly and applied pressure to the wound with his dominant hand, while freeing a hot poker from near the hearth fire with the other.

"Forget this place, Kabili," he said, "or I will thrust this into your wits, so you have no choice."

Kabal laughed heartily. "Bleeding to death and making idle promises? I challenge you to see the end of that threat, prophet. And my name is *Kabal.*"

At that, the fastenings of Kabal's armor loosened and the metal apparatuses struck the ground. Now standing in underclothes, he reached down to recover his belongings but they vanished into the dust. As he knelt, he looked up and discovered that Auni threatened him with his own dagger.

"I have forgotten more about *Njia* than you have ever

known, Kabili. Leave here and forget this place. . .me and the boy."

"Boy?" Kabal looked his former master in the eye. Auni's attempt to erase his memory failed. "Impossible! You went through the rituals, all of them, of that I am certain. Unless. . ."

Auni reeled, realizing that the man previously had no knowledge of Chimelu. "My son. I am his father."

A knowing glance cast itself over Kabal's face. "Please. You would not know what to do with a woman. Your hesitation betrays you. *Mkombozi* lives! After I slay you, he will follow."

Outside, a rabid cub skulked a few feet away from Chimelu. Naked and frightened, he froze as Auni had instructed him to do in the face of a predator. The animal moved closer, as if it decoded the strategy. Inside, Chimelu sensed a darkness feathering the edges of his soul. The bear bore its blood-soaked, sharp teeth and growled terribly.

"Father," he called out. Chimelu slowly stood, reached for the animal skin hanging over the side of a nearby branch and wrapped it around his waist.

Agitated, the bear reared on its haunches, mouth foaming, preparing to strike. Chimelu held his hand out in protest. It snarled, but did nothing else.

As Chimelu stepped gingerly out of the water, the animal leaped forward.

Almost by instinct, he sidestepped the beast – somehow catching it by the mouth – and pried the jaws open. By wrapping his legs around its body, Chimelu immobilized it enough to keep its thrashing to a minimum. He then forced his hands apart until the tendons popped in its jaw.

Now harmless, the cub whimpered on its side. Chimelu relaxed and shoved the animal away from him. He must tell his master, who would be pleased with the victory. Turning toward the hut, Chimelu's mouth dropped in shock. The western side of the hut burned freely, sending acrid black smoke into the sky.

Both Kabal and Auni sensed desperation; the former to follow through and the latter to preserve Chimelu's life. His erstwhile trainee would never leave a task undone. It was this determination to finish that he gambled on in setting the hut ablaze. Should he now die, Kabal would go down to the grave with him, saving Chimelu's identity.

Auni defended himself admirably for a man his advanced age, deflecting most of whatever burning object Kabal had summoned to throw at him, despite his wound. He even mounted a reasonable offensive. But the soldier, weary of fighting at a distance, rampaged through everything in the way and approached Auni, who took to using the poker to block Kabal's sword. It thrust and swung with fury, clanging against equally resistant metal. The cleric stood his ground until Kabal unexpectedly sent a fist across his jaw. Auni dropped the poker and when he reached out his hand to summon it back, the soldier slashed the arm almost through to the bone.

"Now, heal yourself," he mocked.

Auni screamed and dropped to his knees. Pushing past the pain, he retreated inward and focused on collapsing the hut's roof.

Kabal's sword struck just before the roof dropped.

Chimelu's father figure predicted this day.

"At the stroke of tragedy," he had said, "you will leave all you know. Do not look back. Venture toward the direction of the rising sun and ask for an Uché woman named Isoke, the wife of Aitan. Identify yourself to her only."

Quickly, Chimelu donned his dirty clothes and hurried to his burning home, shouting "Father!" over and over again. Nothing inside the conflagration moved. Chimelu circled the area, looking for any sign of life.

*Thump, thump. . .thump, thump. . .*

He heard a heart, at least he imagined the erratic pounding in his inner ear was a heartbeat. *Is it that of my master, or another beneath the rubble?*

"Father!" Brushing aside the ash pasting itself to his brow, Chimelu continued calling. He feared the obvious and wept. *How can I survive the journey northeast on foot without his guidance?*

"Over there!"

Chimelu took cover before Kabal's unit assembled around the fire. The second-in-command assessed the situation at hand, ordering his subordinates to fill their wineskins with water and put out enough of the blaze to enable a search.

"Sir," one protested. "With our numbers and so few skins, a fortnight will pass. . ."

"Then let it pass!" The soldier refused to acknowledge the feeble request with even a look. "Be about it or two moons may pass before my *anger* cools."

The soldier acquiesced. *In truth,* thought the commander, *Kabal would not have even bothered to spit on the fire for any of us! Had we not obeyed orders, and just waited at a distance so Auni could not sense our presence, this would not have happened.*

Nearly an hour later, the men had at least doused the larger flames and begun carefully picking through the rubble. Though their armor protected them from immediate harm, continual exposure to the heat made their mail and helmets unbearable, so they rotated in two-man groups.

"Sir," said one. "We found the severed head of an old man."

He nodded. "Bring it to me."

"Both are dead, sir."

"Very well." The commander's face dropped. "Round up the chariots and let us leave before dusk settles.

Muuaji will be pleased with the treasure."

As they mobilized, Chimelu peeked out from behind a wild bush, moving just enough to attract the attention of the commander.

# ELEVEN

## THE LAST DAY OF FLOOD SEASON, 17 YEARS INTO ENSLAVEMENT, 20 A.B.

Though Muuaji disgusted her, Penda continued sexually appeasing the king at his command, but did so with an ulterior motive. *He will pay for enslaving my people, my family – even if it means sacrificing my own life.*

"If it pleases you, reveal your thoughts, my king," she said with false fervor.

His favorite concubine stroked the fine contours of his darkened forehead. The disturbing news that his former guardsman perished in pursuit of the hermit cleric troubled him like waters stirred during a windstorm. True, Kaizari likely would restore to him a combined kingdom, at least for a few years until Kabal's son was of reasonable age to assume it. But his death confirmed a longstanding known fear of his father's and his own private suspicions that the clerical order may have survived beyond Auni. Though an inspection of the young man they captured revealed that he was not a eunuch, it did little to assuage his concern.

As he and Penda lay, harpists filled the throne room with melodies in attempts to soothe his spirit, for it would be nothing for him to fly into a fit of irrational rage. Only physicality with Penda seemed to calm him. None of his wives or concubines bothered to go into him, for she exerted a strange influence over his emotions.

"This man," he said, stroking his beard. "Remind me of the prophecy again; do not deny me in this. Your sacred texts profess that his bones cannot be broken?"

Penda sighed. "There are no sacred texts. My lord, as I have told you before. . ."

"And as I have commanded," he said, sitting up. "Answer me wisely."

"Forgive me. If it pleases you, I will tell you again all I know of *Njia.*"

Satisfied, he resumed his reclining position.

"*Njia* and prophecies of The Deliverer are little more than passed down memories. Only the clerics had firsthand knowledge, and they refused to inscribe it again after the sack of the temple. Auni was the last to remain of the old clerical order; no other escaped your mighty sword."

*This boy still lives and he may be a disciple.* "So, what is *Njia?*"

"Before the recording of time, the Uché believe EL created this realm. In it, he set what one would call *laws* to govern the movement of humanity. These laws were spoken chiefly to the eleven principle clerics and became known as *Njia.* In Uché, it means *the way and power in which all things are ordered and arranged.* Knowledge of these laws enables one to manipulate how they work."

Intrigued, he repositioned and looked her in the eye. "Tell me of your home, your *true home*, if it is not of this realm."

"No one with a memory of it lives," she said, a hint of sadness dotting her thickly-curled lashes. "Not even Mosi himself knew."

"And what of this *Son of Mosi?* How can he be a son when the father, nor his descendants, live?"

"It had been foretold that a fatherless descendant of Mosi would open the Revelation Gate to reconnect us to EL and establish the way to return home. I do not know how he is to be conceived with no father . . . lest it be by EL, himself."

Muuaji returned to toying with his beard. "Show me the power of *Njia.*"

Penda's eyes searched the room for something to prove her point. She concentrated her sights on the fruit inside a bowl stationed near the bedside and outstretched her hand in a cup, fingers slightly extended. A peach wiggled a bit before lifting from its position, slowly wobbling across the room until it rested in her palm. Muuaji took the peach and examined it, as if it were a fine jewel.

"I imagine Zarek could do the same," he said, tossing the fruit onto the floor. "But you intrigue me. Satisfy your king by teaching him this craft."

She shook her head in protest. "For the little I know Master? It cannot be done."

Muuaji snatched her arm. "*All things are possible. Your* people believe this."

"For the *Uché*," Penda stuttered, writhing in his grasp. "You must be of Uché blood to use *Njia*, even a little bit. It is foolishness to Otī and most Sanguë, though they can learn it also."

Muuaji smacked her across the mouth twice. "Away from me!"

Bleeding from the lips and disgraced, Penda attempted to gather her clothes but was rebuffed. She fled naked from the room, dragging her bedclothes behind her. *He will call for me later,* she thought, *and though it may cost me my life, I will not answer.*

Repulsed, Muuaji turned over and robed himself. He resolved to go to the Uché man and test him before executing him.

Chimelu had finished his third tumbler of water when his armed guardians questioned him again. Other than unusual wit, he was unremarkable.

"Was the eunuch your father?" one asked in jest. Chimelu made no reply, embarrassing his questioner and drawing jeers from his companions.

Another drew a dagger and held it beneath the boy's throat. "The dead fail to answer, as well."

"And how would the king feel," asked Muuaji while entering the room, "if you killed his distinguished guest

and spilt his blood on the ground before they met . . .
where food is prepared, no less?"

The soldiers snapped to attention. Muuaji dismissed
them. "Leave us. The day a slave does me harm is the day
I fall on my own sword!"

The soldiers left, laughing into the vestibule.

"I am called Muuaji by your people," he spoke in
Chimelu's language, "a god among men and ruler of all I
survey. You are to kneel in my presence. Did not the
cleric teach you this?"

He shook his head. "I know to kneel before no one but
EL."

"Of course! I remember tales of his insolence. But you
would bow before an invisible being, and not before *me*, a
*visible god*, in whose presence you now sit?"

Chimelu nodded.

Muuaji chuckled. "I see Auni has passed
stubbornness onto you. Continue and your head may
decorate my throne room with his. And so, what should I
do with you?"

Sadness coated Chimelu's face. "I would ask that you
allow me to go to my people and become one like them."

"Then answer this: You have lived 15 or 17 years,
have you not?"

Chimelu sensed something in the rolling beadiness of
Muuaji's eyes – the same he had seen in the rabid animal
a few days ago. "I remember only 16 years. Father did not
tell me my age, nor of my family."

"But you are *Mkombozi* and are without father."

"*Mkombozi* is unable to be hurt. Look at my skin. I
have bruises and scars. Surely, you know the prophecies,
oh wise Muuaji?"

Confusion flooded the leader's mind. "You would
mock me, little one?"

"Are you mightier than *EL*? Should man fear you, who
can only kill once?"

"And kill at once, I shall!" Muuaji summoned the
guard. "Take him to the empty cistern outside the city.

Death is sure to visit you this night, young one."

The Otī dug their cisterns 20 feet deep; a dry one would likely have a bedrock foundation. The fall alone would break his legs and, if death did not take him through exposure or shock from the injuries, he would starve to death or be eaten alive by ravenous rats. Chimelu shuddered, as the men grabbed his arms and dragged him from the room yelling and screaming.

From the back stairwell, Penda caught sight of the young man glancing at her, as they took him. Recognizing her as an Uché, he mouthed a few words to her. She understood, but turned away, for the word evoked painful memories of her former life.

At that point, she knew what she must do.

Muuaji had rid himself of her and likely would call for another girl, if the needful lust for one arose. Though she would be whipped for her actions by the eunuch assigned to her, she shed the rings in her ears and nose, scrubbed the colored paint from under her eyes and around her cheeks, and tied up her straightened hair in a scarf. Stripped of these trappings and with her raped hair hidden, Penda thought she may again be accepted. The problem was, she could care whether or not the Uché embraced her or not, which made the plan slightly more ridiculous. Anyone sensitive to *Njia* could detect the duplicity with ease.

Still, his plight impressed urgency in her heart, pushing past any reluctance to face the inner demons looming from her past. *If I do not go, he will die miserably.*

"Penda!" A slender hand snatched her shoulder. "Do you not know the hour? Master will have your head!"

". . . if he finds out. Which he won't, Sifa, because you saw me." Penda pulled her fellow concubine aside. "You saw me . . . in my bed . . . because I ate a poorly cooked piece of meat. Nothing to be worried about, just something I need to sleep off. Cover for me and I will return before the last watch."

"The *last* watch?" Sifa's eyes narrowed. "What are you

plotting dressed *like that*?" She paused. "My husband is no more and the king did not wait a night to allow me mourning before claiming me for his. I doubt even my son lives. Let me go, too."

"Not this time. Just trust me. Someone's life depends on it. Speak no more."

At that, without hesitation, she exited from the side entrance closest to the concubine quarters. A harsh, driving rain nearly blinded her. Penda layered her shawl across her face, just enough to keep out the water. After slipping past the distracted night guards, she journeyed adjacent to the merchant road, as the indigent preyed on night travelers too naïve to know any different. She kept her hand at the knife strapped to her thigh – just in case. *Make a move,* she thought, *and give me an excuse.* Returning to her people provided her enough vitriol without extra motivation. The way they treated her – like a *leper* – though she had done nothing to deserve it. She did not surrender as much as *let go*; if not, the thing she treasured most would have torn.

Penda gnashed her teeth and pressed forward. No others dared enter or leave the slave territory during the flood season rains. With no other recourse, she resolved to place one foot in front of the other. Sooner or later, she would stumble upon a home or building and rely on the hospitality of whomever would show her kindness.

A gentle hand cupped around her elbow. Startled, she drew her blade.

"Come," said a man's voice. "Do not be afraid. Let me help you on your way."

Something in his demeanor soothed the fear in Penda's heart. "Do as you will."

He reestablished his hold, this time at her forearm, and led her through the storm. Though terrible thoughts filled her imagination – *he could be leading me to my death,* she thought – even the evilest of men could not fulfill such a desire during a tempest. The pair exchanged no words. As if commanded to do so, upon their arrival, the gates to the slave encampment opened at their approach.

Inside, she wondered who and what lay in store for her, should she ever arrive. Through various officers and servants, she monitored the remnants of her former life undetected. Her husband had died, as prior to the enslavement, his belongings had been transferred and sold. But, her sister remained and her children, as well. All, except the one.

"Here." Penda's escort pointed her toward a small, dimly lit hut straight ahead. "It seems you will find hospitality here."

"Thank you." She curtsied slightly at the knees. "Whom may I say sent me?"

"No need." He waved his hands and left so quickly, that Penda could not determine in which direction he departed.

Penda called out a common greeting and identified herself by her former Uché name. The door swung open and before she could react, a pair of rough hands yanked Penda inside, swung her around and held a sharp object at her back.

"By one notion," her assailant seethed, "you may be considered brave to traverse a night like this. On another, only a fool would come here and use *that name.*"

"It is *mine,*" she quivered, dropping her shawl. "I swear it on my life."

"Then swear it also on the names of *your* children, impostor and prove it!"

"And have their blood spilled? *Never.*"

The metal moved from Penda's back to her stomach. "Theirs or *yours.*"

Penda gasped. "Madiha, the eldest, and Sakina. And Gamba, who is no more."

The knife dropped to the floor and Penda turned to face the person who threatened her. It was a *woman;* bald, but familiar looking, particularly at the aged eyes. Saying nothing, they moved closer together and studied one another. Though soaking wet and purged herself of all things Otī, the body piercings and years of treatments on her tanned skin left her unmistakably *foreign*. Her limp, heat-treated hair was bone straight and little traces of an Uché accent remained. She covered her body modestly – to survive the trip unmolested, no doubt. But she appeared uncomfortable wearing so many clothes, although the weather dictated that she do so.

"Dear sister," said Penda, "it truly is me."

Isoke huffed and set a pot over the fire. It was customary to offer a visitor victuals and water to wash their feet. Due to the late hour, Isoke had no food prepared, but she threw some fresh wood onto the dying embers, stoked it ablaze and tossed some pungent herbs into the pot.

Penda wrung out her headscarf and sat, expectantly kicking off her thongs. Had it not been for the telling eyes, she would not have recognized Isoke. Her curled locks, which at one time in youth fell to the middle of her back, had been cut to the length of a man's fingernail. Small scars were scattered along the sides of her face. These women, once kindred spirits, now treated each other as little more than enemies.

"You have answered well," said Isoke, while pouring her guest a wooden tumbler of strained mango juice, "but the one of whom you speak is long dead. Rest yourself by the fire a while, as the water heats."

Penda moved closer. "Surely then, you recognize my voice. Look in my eyes and seek truth, dear one. See your Mairi standing before you once again, *alive*."

Inside, Isoke knew the truth, but denied it. Pursing her lips, she stared a hole into the floor. "The rains have slowed. Have your drink and be on your way."

"Is there no portion of love in your heart for me, dear one?"

Careful not to awaken her sleeping housemates, Isoke lowered her voice and indicated that Penda should do the same. "You have been living in luxury *all this time – 25 years*! You could have sent word."

Penda composed herself. "Send word? For what. . .to have Aitan exile me again?"

"At least to let me know that you were alive! I grieved for *you*. I married him for *you*. You could have been here, with us, all this time. Your daughters are grown and used for breeding. My son is dead and I am alone. But you have lived *the life*."

"And alone you will be forever, if you do not come with me now. . .you and some men. An Uché will die in a dry cistern if we do nothing."

"Uché perish every day by the hands of your benefactors, while you and your traitorous kind lounge in comfort, your every desire tended to. What is *one* when scores of skeletons litter the river's shore, including that of your son and my own?"

"Bitter shrew," said Penda through clenched teeth, "Chimelu *lives*. Examine your soul and you will know it to be true. *He* is the boy for whom we will seek."

Isoke slapped her soundly across the cheek. "Liar! You are still crazed."

"He said your name to me before soldiers took him away. He will die. If we make haste, he may be rescued; that is, if you have finished admonishing me like a child."

*Chimelu is still alive? Considering his miraculous conception, it may be possible,* Isoke thought. "Leave for your golden palace and become as dead to me as you were before. Your people set traps for us and kill for sport. This is no different. I will not jeopardize my life on a whore and my selfish whims."

"My own life is jeopardized!" she said, tearfully, ". . . have you seen what they do to women? Should Muuaji discover me missing, my fate would be the same, or worse than yours *and* your son's."

"Then why sacrifice your life to come here at all?"

"You know why, as well as I do." She cast her old friend a knowing glance.

"And you believe in *Mkombozi*?" Still wary, Isoke donned a shawl and a walking stick that she used to support her aching knees, as well as for protection.

"Why else would I be here?"

The men, some already in their beds at this point, would not be pleased. Besides rousing them from well-needed sleep, she had allowed a traitor to enter their midst and establish contact with a member of their militia. At the very least, she knew that they would require Penda's eyes or the tip of her tongue as insurance of her loyalty.

"Muuaji will discover you gone tonight, as there will be no return."

The pronouncement hit Penda's stomach like a swallowed stone. A void had enveloped her soul for years, but the pleasures she had experienced at royal hands nipped at it enough to keep her sane. *Without them, what will become of me?*

"Then forget I ever came and bid me leave."

Isoke grabbed Penda's arm as she turned to exit. "You would leave and sentence a man – my son or another's – to *death*? If you are who you claim, and he who lives is my son, you would never inflict that upon me!"

"And why would I not, sister?" She snatched herself free. "Why should I lay down my life to save your child when no one did the same to save *mine*?"

"You are not the only one with something to lose! I may very well be killed for opening the door to you." Isoke lowered her voice. "If your heart still hardens and you believe him to be *Mkombozi*, one day, whether you want him to or not, he will sacrifice all to save *you*. I have no such hope. But you . . . you made your decision when you left the comforts of your chambers to come here. Be sure of this . . .you will not set foot from here alive unless you lead me to him."

Penda nodded in assent and returned to her seat without a word. Isoke emptied the pot above the fire into a foot basin and placed it at Penda's feet. Usually, a host would offer a guest lukewarm water to cleanse their feet after a long walk. However, she preferred it as hot as she could stand due to a strange affliction of the joints that she suffered from. After dipping her toes in for a few seconds, Penda submerged both feet and laid her head back in relaxation.

Suddenly, the door swung open and a unit of armed men entered, startling Penda. Fola, their commander, threw water on the corner of the hearth, extinguishing the peculiar colored smoke trail rising into the air.

"Have you come without Letsego?"

"*This* is your emergency, showing generosity to a *harlot*? Letsego sleeps."

"Then close the door behind you and order your men back."

Fola did as she asked. "Now speak swiftly, for the hour is late."

"Hello Fola," said Penda. "I see that you are still impatient and rough."

He fixed his eyes upon the stranger. "Do I know of you, *traitor*?"

"The *traitor* will lead us to my son," Isoke responded. "I bore a son the day the earth moved and we immediately went into hiding. My all accounts, he should be near 19 years old. You must trust in me that I would not bring our people harm with this. Come with us to save him, so that he may not die."

"This is a fool's errand," Fola replied. "Even if what you say is true, your mission reeks of desperation and our men will not dedicate themselves in its pursuit."

"They will if you convince them to do so. Have you known me to be a desperate fool, brother? Am I not ruled by reason at every mark? I tell you, my son lives. I aim to go . . .with or without your aid."

"Then go!" Fola turned his back and ordered the company out, "and EL's mercy be upon you! There is no glory to be had. No man will accompany you on this suicide errand."

Penda turned toward her former friend. "By their words," she said, "the glory of the Son of EL will come and two women will be his earthly heralds."

Without hesitation, the royal guardsmen assigned to carry out Chimelu's execution unsealed the well, tossed him in and sealed it shut.

The lid had been carved from limestone and moving it out of its fitted groove again would take an extraordinary effort. Besides, if neither the fall nor the rats did him in, he would soon go mad in the darkness or starve to death.

*Why waste time waiting for the inevitable?* Rather than stand guard for a watch in driving rain, each went to their own homes and drank wine to their heart's content. All promised to return in the morning and retrieve the child's body.

Chimelu tumbled down, down, faster it seemed than possible, his back parallel to the ground. He flailed, even extending his limbs out to try and slow his descent, but the circuit of the cistern was too wide and his ability to propel with his mind did not apply to his body. Any second now, the small funnel of moonlight provided by the opening in the lid would disappear, signaling the end of his journey. He would land on the hard floor and shatter his spine, likely along with several other bones.

He closed his eyes, resigned to his fate, and waited for the impact. Afterwards, if not in shock or unconscious, he would struggle for his last breaths, as tiny sets of vermin teeth would aggressively gnaw away his flesh. Whatever was left of him, his capturer made his intent clear – he would place his head on display in front of the slave quarters, alongside that of his father. *Then, who among them would hope for deliverance at the Son of EL's hands?*

Barely a finger's length from the rugged cistern floor, a gentle force caught him at the elbows and at his feet. All Chimelu sensed now, for he refused to reopen his eyes at this point, was a warm presence and the sensation of the rock against his bare feet – he had landed upright! *Did I stop myself from falling? Can I propel myself after all?* If that were true, he could escape? Eyes still closed, Chimelu bent down and jumped as high as he could, only to come back down as fast.

"Not now," said a throaty baritone, "but someday you will walk along the skies."

A startled Chimelu let his eyelids open. Next to him shone an ethereal light so bright that he shut his eyes again and fell to his knees in reverence – just as Auni had instructed. He was in the presence of a herald – a messenger of EL. They were to be respected and feared, for EL gave it orders to announce news or to accomplish a mission, no matter what stood in its way.

"Arise, Son of EL, and do not fear. Gaze upon me once more."

Chimelu dared to look once more. The messenger's glow had dissipated to a tolerable, whitish blue aura that lit and warmed the makeshift cell like a torch. He was of remarkable appearance – like the Uché in his light complexion and long limbs, but more physically menacing than any man he had ever set eyes upon. A fearsome sword hung from a strap at his left side and letters in a strange looking language were inscribed on his belt. He bent on one knee – which placed him about two arm's length taller than the standing boy – and bowed his head in respect. "At your service, my Lord."

"It was *you* who saved me?"

He looked his charge in the eye. "I am your protector, called Mlinzi. Do you hunger or thirst?"

His stomach had been rumbling all through the night. "Both."

Mlinzi spoke in a language Chimelu did not understand. The rats in the well assembled into a group, scurried up the earthen walls to the top and squeezed through the tiny hole in the lid. Seconds later, the herd returned to the well and laid choice bits of meat and bread at Chimelu's feet. Before he could utter protest – for anything touched by a ceremonially unclean animal was forbidden by Uché law to touch – Mlinzi gathered the food and said a blessing over it. As he held it in his hands, he glanced at Chimelu, who sensed it was now safe to consume. And he did so, ravenously devouring all that the herald held out to him. Without a further word, Mlinzi struck the cistern wall with his fist. A stream of water shot out and Chimelu rushed to it, gulping until he had drank his fill. At that, the flow ceased.

"You have rescued me once more," Chimelu said, wiping his sleeve across his mouth. "If it pleases you, save me from certain death and remove me from this place."

"Not at my hands, my Lord, but you will not see death this good night." Mlinzi vanished into thin air, leaving nothing behind but a brief column of light.

"Wait! Stay!" Chimelu dropped his head in disappointment. He reached his hands out and walked back in the opposite direction where Mlinzi had loosed the spring. There, he felt the cold hardness of the earth and clawed at it until he established a hold for both of his hands. He pulled himself up. Before he could gain more ground, the earth dislodged in a clump and he slid down to the bottom. The cistern had been dry for so long that there would be no way he could climb it.

Thus, he brushed his hands off and sat down, his back against the wall, and waited. Some time passed and he fell into several fits of sleep – for how long, he was not sure, as the chill of the night air against his wet body kept him uncomfortable. The moon did not move and by the time a decent trail of light hit the cistern, it would be the second watch and his captors would have returned. If he would be saved, his deliverer must come before then. Should the royal guard find him still alive, Muuaji would be convinced of his divinity and even more determined to kill him.

Chimelu's leg had gone numb. He shifted his position

and the rats scampered away. *Strange,* he thought. He moved his other leg and they retreated yet again. After propping himself up, he hobbled forward and, though he saw next to nothing, he heard movement in the darkness. It was as if the vermin were under strict orders not to touch him. Though he started to thrash around wildly swinging his limbs in every which way, not a ragged tooth, furry tail or coarse hair brushed him. *Mlinzi was gone, but indeed, I will live the night by his words.*

The sounds of intense labor and rock scraping against itself came from high above him. *The lid is being moved! Have my captors returned early?* Chimelu backed against the wall as close as possible, for if the cover were only shifted, he would not be seen. But, not only was it shifted, it was moved completely off its track! *There is no hiding now, for any soul can see me with an adequate light source.*

A considerable time passed. He wanted to look up but did not dare, fearing the inevitable – the dark, round faces of the Otī guard and Muuaji's wicked grin staring back at him. Tears of doubt and defeat rolled down his cheeks.

"Chimelu?" Gravelly but gentle, a female voice called from the opening. Without further hesitation, he looked up to see a strangely familiar face gazing down at him.

Soon thereafter, a rope lowered. Chimelu clutched the line, and, with all his might, began to climb.

# TWELVE

## THE FIRST DAY OF HARVEST, 17 YEARS INTO ENSLAVEMENT, 20 A.B.

**L**ong before the first signs of morning streaked across the horizon, a patrol of Otī footmen marched across the soggy plain toward the well. It searched for the first platoon that had been dispatched a watch ago, but had yet to return.

Since the storm died down not too long ago, it provided a perfect cover story for a night of late carousing. The king did not particularly care – no one could have traversed the area anyway and the cistern was at least three times the boy's height. His body held great interest for the first unit of men, as its retrieval meant riches and lifetime exemption from taxes – an honor bestowed upon those who found much favor with Muuaji. With such an easy assignment, no wonder the men probably engaged in much revelry, which explained why the squadron had not returned to the palace.

Upon reaching the makeshift tomb, the second unit burst out in laughter. Their drunken comrades had passed out around the well, some face down in the dirt, their wine wasted. They approached. Flies alighting upon the bodies failed to stir them. The group drew their weapons and cautiously approached the area. The crimson liquid on the ground was *blood*. Every man had perished a victim of the sword – except one, who stumbled into the well in search of the boy and been eaten in places down to the bone by rats.

Because these men feared EL, they ventured to the Valley of Bones and selected a plausible body, as the bodies had yet to be burned. Most were too small to match those of an 18-year-old man, so the men smashed longer legs and brought back a comparable head eaten past the point of recognition. The caravan carried their fallen comrades and the remains out in the open en route back to the palace, drawing a trickling of Otī townspeople. The word began to spread about the supposed invincible Uché savior that had been killed. His remains were to be strung up on display and Muuaji pledged to make soup from the bones to feed the slaves whom he starved.

Letsego, whom Muuaji permitted to stay inside the palace for a night, heard the whispering and wondered if it could possibly be true. Stirring from beside the concubine that Muuaji had lent him, he covered himself and tip-toed toward the door. Indeed, the king did execute the boy from the wilderness captured two days ago by tossing him inside an empty cistern. *Perhaps now,* Muuaji *shall fulfill his promise to exalt me!*

"Return to me," the concubine slurred. "The sun yet chooses to wake."

He hurried to the bedside. "*Mkombozi* is no more! I shall be set into an office soon, that of a tax collector – no, those men are despised. Something loftier. . .Aitan's chief scribe position, or that of a legislative aide. Adviser to the king! I shall sit at his right hand and grant him wise counsel. My influence shall stretch throughout the lands, perhaps even to the *kusini mwa watu*. Kaizari, himself, will request an audience with me. And you shall be in *my* harem, to pleasure me, not Muuaji.

"Oh, dear brother," he spoke toward the ceiling. "Aitan, if you did not ridicule me and treat me as the younger, not the older. . .you might share, now, in my glory. My riches will eclipse every coin you ever owned in a year's time. Whether you dwell with EL or down in *Kuzimu*, live or die, I no longer care. Another king shall sit on the Uché throne and his name shall not be Muuaji, Kabal, or *Mkombozi*, but Letsego!"

As the news spread throughout the palace to the harem's dwelling place, Sifa hustled to her friend's bed pad and violently awoke her. Startled, Penda unsheathed a knife and swung it in the girl's direction, close enough to catch her robe at the midsection.

"Penda," she shrieked. "Shall you kill me before I bear you news?"

She turned over, her back facing Sifa. "Let me rest, Sifa. I have not slept well. Has the sun even chosen to rise?"

"No, but maybe this will help you slumber better. The Uché boy savior is *dead*. I know you. Do not even pretend that you care."

"*Could it be?*"

"Mmhmm. The men return with his bones, as we speak. I imagine the vermin in that old cistern had a good time picking them clean."

*Something does not make sense,* she thought. *Not only did the boy make it out of the well alive, but I saw Isoke take him in the direction of the slave encampment.* "Are you certain it is *him*?"

"As certain as one can be by the bones of the dead." The girl traipsed off. "*Simama!* The king will want to celebrate with feasting and he will want you to be there! His anger with you will have cooled. And, if you please him, he will not bother *me*."

"It is joyous to know of your concern for me. I shall . . ." Penda paused at the laments filling the air in the Uché tongue from those who still held out hope for *Mkombozi*. Not long thereafter, applause and cheers by their enslavers overcame them, as the troop had arrived.

Not all rejoiced, however, for they also bore the bodies of the men who had killed themselves to avoid the king's wrath. If only he knew those men discovered the makeshift tomb was *empty* upon their arrival!

Still barely dawn, the unit laid both the ashes and the dismembered body at the king's feet on the palace steps.

Muuaji picked up the head, placed his crown on it,

and lifted it high enough for all to see. "Behold, the savior of the Uché! *Mkombozi*, my highly-exalted adversary," he proclaimed with contempt. "Let us feast in commemoration of this day, today and forevermore. Have the cooks slaughter fattened calves and swine. Bring out the best palm wine. Invite Kaizari and let us make preparations to receive him. Soon, this world will belong to the Otī! And this. . ." he said, flaunting the head. ". . . hang this in front of our gates until it is dust. Slay anyone who touches it!"

Isoke idled over a half-eaten bowl of porridge, while Chimelu eagerly devoured his.

The awkwardness of the situation perplexed the boy, who never knew a *woman*, much less a mother. Unlike his fantastical impression of what the opposite sex may be like, Isoke's hair was much shorter than his and she was not lovely, nor soft. Something had beaten femininity far from her and she did not seem to miss it. She smelled of hard work and rain, and treated him not unlike Auni did – lovingly coarse.

Late last night, they exchanged few pleasantries while trekking back to Isoke's hut. She noted that he spoke with humility and eloquence – unlike Auni, who was brusque and rude. Still, she felt as if she walked with EL, himself. For her, fascination with his supposed divine nature bordered on obsession; far above the strangeness of facing her presumed dead offspring for the first time in 17 years.

*Is he Mkombozi, the long-awaited king, who will establish a peaceful kingdom? If so, he can give me answers before I pose the questions.* She dipped her utensil into the bowl. "How is it? And how did you rest?"

"Good," he mumbled between mouthfuls. "Good."

"I make it myself. It is ground maize, with a little cane for taste. It is mostly what we get to eat, except with other meals, it is called porridge and is not sweet. Sakina and

Madiha used to take a liking to it. They would be as kin to you. I raised them as mine own, but they are the daughters of Mairi. Muuaji traded them away two years ago."

Still buried in his food, Chimelu continued to eat without responding, as the shrill screams of mourning for *Mkombozi* unsettled him. They awoke Isoke's six housemates, who arose and stared at him and then at Isoke, who returned the looks with warnings. She played a part in the underground militia and, by nature, the housemates saw things they should not see and heard discussions they should not repeat. Chimelu was one of those things. But, he could not stay with them in the hut unless the Otī officially arranged him to sleep with one of them.

"He will stay with us," she announced, "but not permanently. Adjust to it. If the Otī come, one of you must pretend to be his arranged lover. But do not touch him."

"It is well," one said. The others agreed.

Though intent in his curiosity, Chimelu averted his eyes so they could change clothes with freedom. In his peripheral vision, he saw dangling breasts and slender buttocks. He closed his eyes until Isoke indicated that they were sufficiently dressed.

"Well, Mairi. . .Penda. . .is the woman you met last night." Her face showed a flicker of a smile. "We will hide you. However, you will be expected to work, as the other boys do."

Chimelu's face grew downcast, as Isoke peppered him with information about assimilating into the slave culture. Though the Otī strictly controlled the male population by keeping a low ratio of men to women, they had not taken a census in a year, so Chimelu could fit in without incident. Still years short of true maturity, Chimelu: a solidly-built young man – would be of interest to them. They would mark him for breeding, and later, may trade him to the *kusini mwa watu*.

To Isoke's surprise, neither possibility alarmed him. *Perhaps our deliverance is nigh?* "When will you do as it has been prophesied you would do?" she asked impatiently. "Surely you know these things!"

"We must be prepared. All you seek will come, but not in the time it takes to boil water. There is much work to be done, but little time for it to be complete."

"Tell me then." Isoke leaned in and strongly placed her hand upon his. "What must be done? *How* must it be done? When will this New Order come to pass?"

Chimelu's head hung forward. Isoke saw hints in his face of the baby that she had sacrificed to help fulfill his destiny.

"What troubles you, Chimelu?"

"Father would know what to say."

"I despised Auni for a long time after that day, but it was the only way for you to survive; I didn't know that then, but I see clearly now what I could not understand." *Auni taught him well, for he is wise beyond his years.* "Come."

The migration of Uché to the work camps began at dawn. Isoke commissioned her housemates to station Chimelu in between them as they walked until they exited the female camp and he could blend in among the others. They did so successfully. Isoke and Chimelu waited for Fola, who customarily escorted his sister.

"Who is *this*?" Fola stared the boy up and down.

"*This* is Chimelu," she said, with a hint of pride. No one outside of her, Aitan, Sakina, Madiha, Bimnono, and Lusala knew of his existence. "My *son.*"

"Your *son?*" Fola leaned in close. "My kin? How? Your condition. . ."

". . . is no more. The harlot and I rescued him from the well last night. No need to apologize for your lack of insight."

The trio walked toward the camps. "They have not taken a census in a while. Kabal is dead. He will slip in unnoticed. They will think the Otī put him in there.

Tonight, he will stay with you, but I will find a hut where he can stay, as he cannot stay in mine when Muuaji allows Letsego to return. If the Otī come in, say that he was sent in to one of the women. Keep his presence *quiet.*"

"*Bimnono* will know," she admitted. "How *quiet* do you think she will be?"

"Depends how long you want to keep him *alive*, if he can be killed. I must keep it, as well. Imagine what this news would do for the morale of our fighters!"

He made a good point. "It will be done as you say," she replied.

"You do talk, do you not?" Fola smiled into Chimelu's face. "Where have you been all of this time?"

"The wilderness, with the cleric, Auni."

"That crazed old man who dwelt in the temple ruins?"

Isoke struck her brother in the ribs and pulled him aside. "Have you forgotten whose head sits in the throne room of our adversary? Auni is the only father he has ever known."

A well-trained soldier lacking diplomacy and tact, Fola apologized and changed the subject. "You will join the boys your age to harvest yams. Your mother will be at the armament camps. Join us at the great stump. We will eat there."

Fola, Isoke and Chimelu folded into the main procession; a funeral march to the work camps. None smiled or particularly frowned, though. Mothers strapped their young – those who could not yet walk – closely to their bosoms for warmth in the early morning and did their best to keep them quiet. The overseers hated noise and an abundance of crying infants could incite them. It would not be the first time.

Chimelu observed the long, gaunt ashen faces and scarred gathering of limbs moving in staggered unison. The men looked to have endured the worst physically, as many of them limped along. Sores and keloids the size of ripe apricots decorated their broad shoulders, the fruit of disobedient actions or the crime of being available. Seeing the elbowed stub of an armless man sent a cold shiver down Chimelu's spine.

Near the produce fields, Fola peeled away. A heavyset woman approached with particular interest in him, as did a girl beside her who was Chimelu's age. She peeked at Chimelu from behind her mother's girth.

"Isoke!" Bimnono said, still staring at the boy. "Who is this?"

Isoke grabbed her arm tightly. "You know very well who this is. Quiet!"

"I knew it! Lusala, this is Chimelu. Chimelu, this is Lusala, and I am Bimnono, her mother. We are your kin . . . in a way."

Lusala's heart jumped at the mention of her childhood friend's name. She threw herself into Chimelu's arms, embracing him tightly.

Isoke separated them before they drew the attention of the Otī. "Have you gone mad, girl? They will kill you both! Mind yourself. And in no way are you kin. I am minding him, while his father is away. That is all you need to know, all anyone needs to know. Say nothing else."

Bimnono pulled Lusala by the hand. "Sanguë are not to be enslaved, but I volunteered. And soon, my voluntary became involuntary. They no longer heed their own laws, but care only that the work is done well."

"Look ahead to the left. Those are the yam fields," said Isoke, pointing to a large area of farmed land. "Beyond those, about a few thousand paces, is where I will be at the armament camps. When the horn blows, meet me and Fola.

"Pick one of the fields, grab a tool and do what the others do. If someone asks who you are, say you are a son of the house of Aitan. Our husband was well-respected, even among the Otī. Use my name, if they inquire further. When we are together, do not speak to me familiarly. Call me Isoke. And, if one named Letsego approaches you, he is not to be trusted. Do you understand these things?"

He nodded and then ran with the others, as the first to the fields claimed the best digging tools. The others had to use inferior tools to dig the tubers loose from the ground. The work was not labor intensive, but time consuming, and the rate at which they were expected to do it was ridiculous – even for an energetic teenager.

He approached the digging implement and handled it with timidity, for Auni used a makeshift version of the same thing, but he had not been permitted to touch it. Chimelu followed Isoke's instructions and struck beneath the soil, as the others did. However, he misjudged the distance underground and pulled up a cut-in-half yam that earned him a backhanded slap from one of the overseers.

After relieving him of the tool, the man asked him the dreaded question. "Just who are you, anyway? I am familiar with all the slaves and do not know you."

Chimelu looked at the ground. "I am of the house of Aitan."

"Are you now?" The man stroked his chin and studied the boy. He pointed to a spot inhabited solely by girls. "Get over there where you can be useful, son of Aitan!"

To be a boy working among girls was a clear mockery of his masculinity, but Chimelu did not mind – at least until he gained a better understanding of what to do and how to do it. As he neared, a couple of girls chuckled, saying things like "here comes another one" and "just what we need." Chimelu stationed himself close to the wheelbarrow where they separated the yam from their leaves. This time, before trying it himself, he watched the movements of their hands until the overseer made it clear that he would be whipped soon for not working. After a while, he was doing the same quality work that the girls did, but almost twice as fast.

"Slow down, will you?" The others had seen enough and appointed Lusala as their spokesperson. "The overseer will think us lazy and make us work harder."

"Should we not serve others the best we can. . .in all circumstances?"

"Who told you that nonsense?" She giggled. "Work fast and they will still whip you, if they feel like it. What difference does it make then. . .whether we try hard or not? The reward is still a lashing!"

Unlike the appearances of the others, Lusala's long, cocoa hair and medium chocolate skin glistening with perspiration entranced Chimelu. Like all Uché/Sanguë cross-breeds, she exceeded her peers in height and her features earned her contempt.

"Why is your hair so long? Have you never dared to cut it?"

He failed to answer that the rites of a cleric included an unshaven head. Instead, he drowned himself in Lusala's darting charcoal pupils. She plucked a yam from the earth and, after handing it to him, cradled his hands in hers. A spark of excitement shot up into his bloodstream.

"See," she demonstrated, pulling the leaves off in a less haphazard way. "The trick is to *look* like you are handling them with care, which you are, but taking more care takes *more time*." She brushed the vegetable clean and placed it in the wheelbarrow. "Try it our way and the others may hate you less."

Later that day, after he met Isoke and Fola for a meal and finished his labor, each encampment broke for the evening. Isoke searched for her son and barely recognized the tanned, soiled being that joined her. She was sure that he would be at the point of collapse after a day's labor, but Chimelu seemed to have almost as much energy as when she had left him that morning. His enthusiasm suffered a blow, however, when Bimnono and Lusala could not be found.

"I see no whip marks on you, so you must not have gotten into any trouble."

Chimelu turned his bruised cheek toward Isoke, who

stopped and handled him at the chin. "It is nothing. It does not even hurt anymore. I accidentally cut a yam in half while digging."

"It was probably rotted through, anyway. The Otī will do as they please, however and to whomever they please, even you."

The two walked in relative silence back to Isoke's hut, where she concocted a stew of broth from animal bones and a piece of meat that she had salted. Chimelu bathed in a wooden tub, not unlike the one he had been used to – except it was inside, much to his delight – while Isoke's housemates ate behind an animal skin that she hung when privacy was essential. After she bathed, the two of them sat to dinner. She invited him to say a blessing over the food.

"Father," he said in reverence, "we remain indebted to you for the bounty you have bestowed upon us today. May your blessing rain down from the other realm, as we partake of this feast. EL be praised."

Isoke did not repeat the blessing, as was customary to followers of *Njia*, but started eating after Chimelu finished. "I would not necessarily call stew a *feast*. Be careful, Chimelu. It is hot."

It was too late, for the boy had blown a spoonful cool, swallowed it, and had almost consumed another.

"You would think you had never seen food by the way you eat."

"Father," he said, still chewing, "Auni could not cook like this. He tried, but. . ." His voice trailed off. He popped a piece of bread in his mouth and chewed contemplatively.

Isoke noticed his melancholy and redirected the conversation. "My mother taught me how. It is nothing, really, but, like anything, a practice in patience and experimentation."

Mother and son sat in relative silence for a moment, save the *clink* of utensil against bowl.

"So, tell me about you and Lusala today. I saw you

two in the fields together."

Chimelu buried his eyes in the rippling liquid inside his cup. The girl's untamed nature had affected him in a mysterious way, and at the mention of her name, his heart fluttered.

"Your feelings for her; I would have chosen another for you, not a half-breed and one a little more respectful. She feels the same for you, I suspect. Bimnono has been trying to arrange her for moons."

"No." Chimelu looked his mother in the eye. "Perhaps she does, but it cannot be. She *is* part-Sanguë and I have already taken the vows."

Isoke guessed as much. As a cleric-in-training, he would have been castrated and thus would have no sexual desire or purpose to marry. *But had he?* She had no intention of physically inspecting him, but his attraction to Lusala suggested otherwise.

"It is natural to have affection towards any girl, as long as you keep them in place. Only the unwise and the unlearned make decisions based on the heart's desires, unsteady as they may be. Union with foreigners is what led to our captivity in the first place."

Unsure whether or not his acceptance of her wisdom was merely an act of tolerance, she cleaned the dishes and gave Chimelu a mat and animal skin to lie on near the fire. He had not felt fatigue all day until he settled in front of the hearth. Before lying down and drawing the skin towards his chin, he knelt and said a prayer. Later, after much tossing, he turned toward Isoke. "Tell me a story. I cannot sleep."

Isoke sat cross-legged at the end of her sleeping space. "Once, I asked my father about the captivity and he told me a story about a man, whom EL found to be more righteous than all. In fact, EL loved this man so much that he named him *Mosi*, for he should become the ruler we had prayed for. Mosi was a *warrior*. Songs about his military successes were sung in the temple all night and day.

Eyes drooping, Chimelu wanted to hear the story's conclusion.

"Mosi's first wife was without child. He took a second and third Uché bride, but still no male heir. He married 13 times and none of his wives bore him a son. Mosi became the scorn of the people and many spoke of his shame publicly, though he could have had them killed. Many suffered his wrath, but the populace looked at him as if it was his fault EL had not opened up their wombs for a male heir.

"Finally, the army journeyed across the District River for battle. Mosi did not go and take his rightful place with the men. Instead, he went about the palace, trying to soothe his wounded soul. The people who once loved him now hated him. During this time, he found a woman more beautiful than all of his wives combined, but she was Sanguë. Back then, to wed a Sanguë would be like marrying a *mbwa mwitu*. It was not permitted. Mosi took the woman as his wife and she bore him two sons. EL struck the first, as he was not to marry a foreigner. Because of this betrayal, the latter stages of his reign led to the sack of Nozi, the death of his line and the captivity of the people."

Chimelu was fast asleep by the end of her sentence, long before the part where the Son of Mosi entered the fabled Revelation Gate to deliver the people.

At dusk that same night, Muuaji stumbled into his throne room with a wine chalice and using an audacious scepter for a walking stick. Raising his glass to toast, he slurred "to *Mkombozi*" and emptied it, before looking to his cupbearer to refill. The cupbearer was nowhere to be seen and he thought to have the man killed, before, remembering that the revelry ended hours ago and that he had given the servants their leave. It was considered shameful to be drunk before them, so he held off during the feast. Muuaji belched and laughed at himself. *If only*

*my father could see me now!* At his favorite window, he peered toward the north gate, where the boy's bones hung.

"See, Father!" he exclaimed. "I mock your enemies. The child you sought to kill is eaten by flies and vultures on my gates and the head of the cleric you could not kill is a preserved ornament! Your enemies are beneath my feet and my kingdom, *not yours*, endures. Do I fail you now? Are you disappointed in the ruler I have become?

"The assistant to one of your most trusted Uché scribes, Letsego, is now my *spy*. He has informed me that, of all the children you killed, you missed *one*, who escaped underneath *your watch*, not mine. Now, he is dead. I accomplished something you could *never do*." Muuaji bowed, as if giving a performance warranting praise. "The people now sing songs of my victories, *not yours*."

*How long will you blaspheme?*

The king jerked his head around at the sound of a voluminous voice. Still alone, he surveyed each entrance and found no one. "Father? Who speaks?" He awaited a response. Convinced he drank too much wine, he placed the chalice at its place near the throne. None of his magicians, not even Zarek, summoned spirits from beyond and the gods in his pantheon did not audibly speak. Still, he set a peace offering before them all and petitioned their forgiveness and favor, as the voice expressed displeasure with him.

Satisfied, he steadied himself from a kneeling position at the altar. If the gods were angry with him, he curried their favor with a fragrant offering, and if the sound came from his imagination, he would sleep off the stupor. The gray head of the cleric caught Muuaji's attention, its haunting glass eyes staring forward. The look was one of peace and contentment, not horror. Several of his courtiers pleaded with him to close the eyelids before preserving it, but he refused, claiming Auni "looked better this way."

*He, whom you sought to kill lives,* said the ethereal voice.

"Identify yourself!" Muuaji armed himself with a short sword that he kept close all times. "Confront me, if you dare. See if I do not rend you stomach to throat."

*He will be of the offspring of the house of Mosi, the Son of EL.*

At the mention of Mosi and the name of EL, Muuaji suspected the severed head of the cleric was the culprit. He touched it with the pads of his fingers. The hardened muscles did not move. He dismissed the voice once again.

*You will mock and accuse him. They will hear him, but not believe.*

This time, Muuaji was looking in the direction of the head and it still did not move. Thinking that it may be the connection, he lifted the head from its place and tossed it with might into the garden.

*His bones cannot be broken. He will heal and raise the dead.*

Somehow, the cleric spoke to him from another realm of Mkombozi. Did the Uché savior live, or did the cleric speak of one to come?

"He lives?" he asked drunkenly to the ceiling, "or does he have yet to be born?"

*He will enter The Revelation Gate and ascend the skies.*

"Answer me, cleric! Does he live, or does he have yet to come? Answer me!"

The disembodied voice said nothing else, though Muuaji begged it to do so. When Kaizari appeared for the feast, they would have a new focus – raise the army they planned, drive the Uché from the face of the earth, and reclaim the next realm for *Adui wa EL*.

# THIRTEEN

## THE FOURTH DAY OF HARVEST, 17 YEARS INTO ENSLAVEMENT, 20 A.B.

After several days of harvest, the work came easier to Chimelu. His muscles toned and adjusted to the demand of digging soil and lifting its produce. But, for the first time, the activity wearied him late that afternoon, attracting the attention of his superior.

"You!" The overseer with skin dark as midnight pointed at him and yelled. "This is not break time. Get back to work, or I will see you whipped by my hand!"

In truth, he had only just laid down his shovel and swiped his brow to give his aching back a chance to stop spasming. Chimelu complied, only to drop the tool again in pain. Though the others noticed, none moved to help him. Such an action would cause lack of production on two fronts and cause them both to be beaten.

The overseer leapt from his perch and approached Chimelu to recompense the insolence. Working a fair distance away, Isoke kept an eye on him. She asked Letsego, who had recently been moved to the same camp, to do so as well, but she did not disclose the new boy's identity to him beyond that of a general interest. He complied, in exchange for an open mouth kiss, which she was loath to grant him.

When the man approached Chimelu, she committed an error in her own work, resulting in a sharp blow to the cheek by her own supervisor. She repositioned herself to monitor him without breaking stride in her duties.

A heavy fist came down upon Chimelu's face, bloodying his lower lip. He spit out a dark red stream and pain shot throughout his bottom teeth. Chimelu balled up his fists, but did not strike a blow. The overseer returned to his shaded seat and ordered all back to work, or they would receive the same punishment.

Isoke breathed a sigh of relief when the man retreated. Yes, her son had been punched, but would live to tell the tale, unlike others who had suffered worse.

Chimelu lifted the tool again and remarkably, the pain had subsided. A cool sensation settled at his brow and washed over him in waves while, all around him, his slave brethren continued sweating in the noon sun. *Could it be Mlinzi?* Curious, he said "Mlinzi" out loud.

"Why do you speak foolishness?" asked a slave digging in the row next to him. "Sing like the rest. Do you not know this one will whip you until your flesh hangs from your bones?"

"Something is happening. Do you not feel it? Look at me. Why do I not sweat in this heat?"

"Because you do not work," he replied. "Dig! Will you be struck again?

The two did not notice the overseer dismount again and approach, whip in hand. He uncoiled it and cracked it loose at the talking slave's back. "Get back to work, all of you, and do not talk!" Another lash freed blood from his stomach and the last, a freakishly violent blow to the center of the face dropped him to the ground in pain. The whipping continued until his body no longer moved.

Horrified, Isoke watched as the man recoiled the whip, this time for her child. Though she knew it would cost her two score lashes, she dropped her work and rushed to the scene. Fortunately, most of the other slaves followed. If they all had to be hit two score times, it would take all day and no work would get done. As the overseers corralled the gathering mob and ordered it back, Chimelu raised his hand. "Whip us no longer, neither me nor the others. We are working to the best of our abilities."

*What impunity?* The man laughed and yanked his arm back. Without warning, he dropped to the soil and did not move. The Otī restraining the slaves witnessed this.

Unbeknownst to all but Chimelu, Mlinzi stood over the offender with his invisible sword buried between the man's shoulder blades.

After turning him over, the Otī determined that his heart had stopped – not terribly unusual, for Otī men lived short lives. The appointed replacement, a man who secretly feared EL and beat only to keep up appearances, removed the body from the field and sent the others back to work. Chimelu informed the man of his injury and he was permitted to clean yams again for the remainder of the day with Lusala.

"So," said Lusala with a smirk, "do you think you can kill our overseer too? I tire of his mouth."

She had mastered how to annoy him over the past few days. "I did not kill him."

"But you did not *save* him. Your people believe in using *Njia* to save."

Chimelu pondered her question. "It was not EL's will for him to be saved."

"How do you know? I thought it was EL's will that *all men* be saved."

"Yes, but you cannot make someone accept something that they do not believe."

"So be it. Whatever grants you peace."

Chimelu absentmindedly kept cleaning yams. "What will become of his mama?" he asked. "He was her only son."

"She will survive." Lusala yanked the leaves of a yam in her hand and tossed its rotten top into the waste pile. "We all do. Your people call us *mbwa mwitu*, but wild dogs do not often die . . . they *fight*."

Chimelu looked at her tenderly. "I never called you a *mbwa mwitu*."

"You do not have to," she said. "Your people think it and I am more Uché than Otī. It hurts to be rejected due to something I have no control over."

The two tended to their work awhile without speaking, for they reached an impasse as they often did. Her

Sanguë-raised mind did not readily accept the truths of *Njia*, so many of their conversations because futile exercises in rhetoric; he presenting a point and she refuting and debating it. He tried to explain, but for his best intentions, they hailed from two different worlds – both literally and figuratively.

Lusala caught him staring at her on more than one occasion, but did not question it until she noticed Chimelu's eyes never relished anything below her neck.

"Is there nothing else that interests you?"

Embarrassed, Chimelu caught himself and blushed. "I apologize."

"About me?" she asked, coyly. "I am used to being stared at, but not for my face. Most Uché girls are pretty poles with nothing to distinguish them from you. Sanguë girls are not as pretty, but have better figures. I received the best of both worlds. But, have your choice of those, if you can distinguish them from the boys."

She leaned far over the wheelbarrow and busied herself long enough for him to look down her dress, but Chimelu did not submit to her wiles, or his own curiosity.

Something about him drew Lusala in. "So, I am to be arranged for marriage by the days of feasting," she admitted. "I suppose I brought this upon myself, but I am not of the stock to be a bride. You are past the age to be arranged, as well, but the Otī only allow Uché to breed and not marry. Even then, Muuaji may trade any of you away. So, why even try?"

Unsure of how to respond, Chimelu said nothing, further inciting her.

"My mama fears I will become a woman of the street, but what is wrong with consorting with someone you care for outside the bonds of marriage? I would rather do so than consort with one and dream of another, like I have heard her say."

He smiled at her and Lusala returned the favor. Auni spoke of his own training when everything tried to deter him. Instead, he shook loose of the distractions and focused on his mission. Chimelu would do the same. He would not touch her tenderly, or sire a family through her. Such things were forbidden. *There can be nothing more between us.*

Isoke's familiar touch rested on his shoulder. "You two have not noticed that the others have gone for the day? They will let us work forever, but it is time to go for the sun is setting when no man can work."

He sighed. "See you tomorrow?"

Lusala nodded. "Be well and I will see you, if the sun chooses to wake."

Isoke waited until Bimnono had taken Lusala out of earshot. "She seems a bit taken with you."

"*Lusala?*" He smirked innocently.

"You have taken vows, none of which involve her. My husband was her father, which makes you almost kin. Yet, she carries on with you as if . . .you *do*, you *enjoy it!*"

Chimelu tried hard to suppress his amusement. "It's *innocent*. Why does it bother you so?"

"It is *inappropriate!* You will be of fighting age at the beginning of summer and must make these decisions for yourself. And that girl is hardly innocent. Bimnono has caught her on more than one occasion. She will be on her back in no time."

Chimelu made note of the date. He had never known his birthdate before. Auni never told him and he never thought to ask, as they did not celebrate or feast in the wilderness. "Do the Uché celebrate their dates of birth?" he asked, solemnly.

"Yes," she admitted, saddened by his inquiry. "Or at least we did before the enslavement. We also feasted on the first days of the year. Now, there is nothing to celebrate." She fanned herself with her hand and took a deep breath.

"When is my date of birth? How old am I?"

Flushed with sadness, Isoke's voice softened. "The third to last day of harvest. We used to count the years from the captivity, but now count from the time of our enslavement, which numbers 17. I bore you two years before our enslavement, so you are 19 years old."

The answer satisfied Chimelu, who counted just another three full moons until his 20th birthday, officially making him of fighting age.

"Watch your conversation, Chimelu. Temptation is a worthy adversary who cleans his teeth on the bones of those who take him lightly."

"You have spoken well, Mama. I will do as you say."

Now allotted a space in one of the settlements for young men, Chimelu acted like the others – as naturally as possible. He bathed after one of the boys bided his time, and he ate as they ate – ravenously, without care for its temperature or lack of seasoning. They only asked his name and house of origin once, for which he replied "Chimelu, of the house of Aitan," thus, levying a degree of respect among them. Even for the following generation, Aitan was revered for the honorable death he had endured rather than to align himself with the Otī or provide them with valuable information.

That night, as he lay on his mat, a voice called his name. A quick survey of the room revealed that all the boys slept soundly. Rather than resume sleeping, he crossed his legs and meditated. The quietness of night or the stillness of morning allowed unparalleled times of concentration and insight into *Njia*. Chimelu fell into a trance so deeply that he ascended to another realm lit with starlight. He had seen this illumination before, but Mlinzi was nowhere within sight. Above him, indescribable beings flew past. If he caught sight of one of them, the words he thought to express dissolved as quickly as they had formed.

Chimelu continued to meditate, practicing patience as Auni had taught him to do when circumstances arose and answers did not readily present themselves. He was unsure of how much time had passed, as the atmosphere did not perceptibly shift. Its air currents felt like water flowing over his body, though it did not require him to hold his breath. Suddenly, his mind was presented an image: a wooden circle with four lines inside it intersecting a central line at two points.

"You are the offspring of the house of Mosi, the Son of EL." Auni said by his soul, which appeared before Chimelu and exhorted him to stand. "They will mock and accuse you, but you will say nothing. They will hear your words, but not believe them. Your bones cannot be broken and you will measure justice to all."

"Who is just, but EL himself?" asked Chimelu. "Who is more just than he?"

"*You* have been chosen to mete justice," the cleric replied. He bestowed a necklace upon Chimelu; a gold representation of the symbol he envisioned bound by a leather thread. "You will enter the Revelation Gate, and ascend the skies."

Chimelu knew many of the prophecies about *Mkombozi* well, but did not understand why Auni's soul did not address him more directly. "What of the Revelation Gate, Father?" Now impatient, he inquired further. "*Where* is it?"

"You must go to it," Auni said coldly. "And you will die for it."

When Kaizari arrived at the Otī palace, days after Muuaji had summoned him, he found the regent passed out. According to the servants, since the death of *Mkombozi*, he had spent the majority of his time this way: unshaven, unbathed, and hurling obscenities. Kaizari snapped his fingers. His servants lifted Muuaji at the arms and dragged him into his bedroom.

"Incompetent fool." Kaizari laid a papyrus scroll on the bed next to Muuaji. "Administers to two-thirds of my kingdom and cannot keep sober." He motioned his hand across Muuaji's forehead and waited.

Muuaji blinked his eyes and sneezed twice before sitting up. "What sort of sorcery have you performed? I feel better than I have in years!"

"You have been drunk these entire four days?" Kaizari, now a master of the Otī language, needed no interpreter. "You should have awakened long ago."

"In honor of the death of my adversary," he said, intentionally omitting the ghostly message, "I sent you word. The harvest is ripe, also. Should I not be merry?"

"You should not for those reasons," he admonished. "The Uché savior lives."

"And how are you certain?" scoffed Muuaji. "Have you seen him?"

"I sense his presence through *Njia ya kifo*. You may have known, as well, if your sensibilities were not drowned in palm wine and merriment."

"And what of the bones I hanged at the northern gates?"

Kaizari sighed. "Frauds. Probably from that valley you throw them in."

Angered, Muuaji cursed and summoned the royal guard. "Bring the heads of those responsible for producing the bones of the Uché boy to me!"

Kaizari rested a hand on Muuaji's right arm. "Respect is not gained through fear, young man. Did you learn that from your father?"

Muuaji raised his hand against Kaizari, but feared that striking the powerful man would not be in his best interests. Kaizari cleared the room of people, except for him and Muuaji.

"Explain this behavior at once, lest I strike you myself."

Muuaji recounted the harrowing experience in the throne room, how the voice of Auni now tortured him day and night, and the only respite from it was subsisting in a drunken stupor where coherent thought was impossible. He repeated its haunting words to Kaizari, who stretched the scroll across the bed.

"Your ancestor did not destroy the prophecies," he explained. "We have preserved them since the eleven fell.

They are what you have heard spoken to you."

"Impossible!" Muuaji huffed in disbelief. "How do you know these to be the *true* Uché prophecies? You could have been defrauded by them, yourself!"

"I helped remove them from the temple prior to its destruction."

The statement gave the Otī king pause. Kaizari looked to be no older than Kgosi would have been, yet he claimed to be more than *eight centuries old*.

"The prophecies are EL's effort to convince the people of this realm to follow him. *Adui wa EL* does not need to resort to such trickery. We follow him willingly, without convincing. EL's deception will culminate in his demise."

Muuaji contemplated this. "These sayings will not come to pass?"

"Do not be deceived. . .there *is* a Son of Mosi," he warned, unrolling the text. "He dwells amongst you and will do the unnatural in your midst."

"If he exists, why not seek and destroy him *now*?"

"There is a time for all things and that time has not come."

"Then *when*?"

Irritated by his impetuous company, Kaizari continued reading. "His bones cannot be broken. The Uché will call him their king and he will enter the Revelation Gate." At that point, he closed the scroll. "After EL's defeat, we will rule this realm and the next with *Adui wa EL* forevermore."

Muuaji salivated at the prospect of governing *territories*. Anticipating the hunger in his eyes, Kaizari fed him another prophetic morsel.

"And when the Son of EL suffers," he said, "his blood will run over your hands."

# FOURTEEN

## THE SECOND WEEK OF SUMMER, 17 YEARS INTO ENSLAVEMENT, 20 A.B.

**O**f all those involved in the conflict, Fola trusted Letsego the *least*. Though the two had shared living quarters since the enslavement began, and Letsego did provide useful intelligence reports regarding the growing strength of Muuaji's armies, something about the glint in the former scribe's eye seemed fraudulent. Or, perhaps it was the manner in which Letsego stared through his sister when her attention wavered elsewhere.

Nevertheless, the others entrusted him, so Fola attempted to bury his misgivings about the upcoming raid on the Otī armory. According to Letsego, with the abundance of weapons in store, they could pilfer enough to weaponize a third of the Uché without notice. He claimed that the guardsman manning late into the third watch was slothful and prone to sleeping on the job. After disposing of him, one would stand guard while the others stole enough to be useful but not to be missed.

The men had followed Letsego's lead many times before and he had never led them astray. Because of this flawless record, they began disregarding Fola's hunches and suggestions, though his background and service merited it.

*They rather follow a scribe who could not lift his own weight, if his life depended on it,* Fola thought. *They will see. He will fail them yet and I will witness it with my own eyes!*

The raid was planned shortly after the Otī stopped manning the settlement gates, as they concentrated their resources on assembling arms and formation of the massive army. In addition to drafting every man of fighting age for service, they trained young boys for the military, as well. This force, unparalleled in the known world, often went on missions to scout and conquer previously unknown lands. Many times, they returned with nothing. Other times, they had confiscated metals, jewels and raw materials the likes of which none of the races had ever seen. And they killed everything that moved. The populace celebrated, feasting with every conquest.

"This vulnerability will prove to aid us," Letsego reasoned a moon ago.

"It is ill-conceived," Fola argued, "and will result in our bloodshed. If we continue our present course, assembling them through the weapon stations, we could do the same in a few moons."

"*A few moons?* Let us go forth and do so, Fola, lest our courage quail further and we be enslaved another 20 years. We have been beaten-down slaves long enough. I will sacrifice my blood to empower my people. Will you swear the same?"

The challenge boiled Fola's insides, as his comrade challenged his manhood in front of the others. Letsego already wore the respect of the men like a mantle and did not need to add Fola's dignity to his wardrobe. "I will be in command . . . in case something goes awry."

"Of course!" Letsego agreed. "I would have it no other way."

And now, as Fola assumed the position of the indolent guard at his post, he questioned Letsego's wisdom once more. As the closest size to the guard's stature and the most experienced in hand-held weapons, Fola was ideal to defend himself in case his identity was uncovered. Conversely, he did not know enough of the Otī language and lingual inflections to portray a convincing fraud. He hoped his countrymen would make haste, for Letsego commanded them inside the armory.

One of the Otī guards waved in Fola's direction. *What can he want?* He came running over to Fola, who took a deep breath and moved away from the mounted torch. Hopefully, in dim lighting, the clay powder caked onto his skin to make him look darker appeared convincing enough through the exposed parts of his armor.

"I have been on for two watches," he said in the Otī language, stopping short of Fola. "Watch my post, while I relieve myself."

Fola understood the words "two watches" and "relieve myself," and assumed the guard asked him to watch his post, so he nodded. The relief area was closer to Fola's post than the other, so it did nothing to allay his nerves. He stuck his head into the storage facility and instructed the eleven men to remain silent until he gave the signal.

When the guard returned, he found Fola feigning sleep on the job, shook his head and resumed his post in the distance. Some time later, Fola gave the signal. One of the men created an ill-directed distraction, drawing the attention of the guard toward Fola rather than away from him.

Fola immediately engaged him, landing a number of blows to his body before thrusting a knife into his chest. "Go!"

Streams of arrows rained in from undisclosed locations, felling half the team. Before Fola could join them, the guard whom he impersonated stuck a sword through his stomach. One of the Uché soldiers turned to see Fola fall and pierced the assailant with a spear guided true though the heart.

"Make haste!" Letsego waved them forward. "Morning is to come and we have sacrificed enough today. Let us not join them in death!"

"We will not!" The spearman and another dropped their armaments and braved through flying arrows to retrieve the limp bodies of the fallen, carrying them the distance back to the slave settlement. As the sun rose over the horizon, all the men of the encampment surrounded Fola's hut in a show of respect for what he and the others had done for the nation.

"One of you who knows his kin," Letsego said, pointing in the direction of the youngest men. "Fetch his sister, Isoke, of the house of Aitan, and make haste!"

After some moments, Fola's breathing staggered. While the others had died, he clung to life.

Isoke pushed past the crowds and knelt at her brother's side, cradling his head in her hands. "Brother," she sobbed, while stroking his head. "First our Hawa, now must I lose you, as well?"

Chimelu emerged beside them and laid a hand on Isoke's shoulder. "It is well. Be comforted."

Isoke clasped Chimelu's hand in hers and looked at him intently. She witnessed him raise the dead before, but as a child, and in secret. *Will he do so openly?* "If you are willing, I implore you to do so."

Chimelu cupped his hand and pressed it over Fola's deep wound. A light like that of the sun shone through the spaces in Chimelu's fingers. All those close to him, particularly Isoke, shielded their eyes. Immediately, the wounded flesh closed up.

Fola gasped for breath and sprung alive. Still shaking with shock, Isoke reached a hand through the fissure of his garment and felt nothing, not even the residual of clotted blood. After withdrawing clean fingertips, she displayed them to the crowd.

A collective gasp sounded throughout the packed hut, as Chimelu performed the miracle again and again by raising every fallen soldier. Those Uché who did not faint, kneeled at his feet, chanting, *"Tazama Mkombozi, Tazama Mkombozi, Tazama Mkombozi,"* which means "Behold, The Deliverer." They surrounded Chimelu, careful not to touch him, for who knew if he could revoke the ability to live as quickly as he granted it?

While he knelt, Letsego placed value on this knowledge and how it may further benefit his standing in the eyes of Muuaji.

Later that day, the Uché sang giddily while working, smiling at their would-be savior. *He will deliver us soon,* they thought. *Perhaps today, or tomorrow, he will save us.* Some plotted revenge on the oppressors who unmercifully flogged them, compiled precious metals and gems in their minds, or wondered how much territory *Mkombozi* would allot them in the New Order. The conquests of the Otī taught the Uché an important principle: the realm's boundaries were much farther than initially thought. Divided equitably, each man may be able to rule over a kingdom larger than his eye could perceive! Nothing, not the labor, whipping, or malnourishment mattered. All that mattered was the glory.

The overseers thought the aliens acted strangely, more so than other days, but did not question it, as the Uché labored without complaint. Although Chimelu's 20th birthday approached, he remained in the fields instead of aiding in construction with men his age. He could have handled the arduous labor, but preferred reaping and sowing. He missed working alongside Lusala and her laconic retorts in their conversations. For now, their time together would be relegated to only meals.

But Chimelu could not be found during the break time. He disappeared without pretense. Fola joined Isoke and Bimnono instead, and Lusala ate with them.

"Where is he?" Bimnono asked, impatiently. "*Everyone* seeks him out. There are rumors that he is the cleric Auni, or even Mosi, come again to life. Of course, I know this is not true, *is it? And* he has vanished. Is that one of his abilities through *Njia?*"

Isoke chewed and maintained her silence on the subjects. Fola did the same.

"Will you not answer me?" Bimnono pressed. *Do they even know?*

"It appears you were correct in your apprehensions, brother," said Isoke, who redirected the conversation.

"Something just does not seem right about it," he admitted. "Everything went according to planned until the distraction was incorrectly placed."

"Who is responsible?"

"None are saying so. I suspect it was the only one among us with no experience. Only a fool would draw enemies toward himself. If not for *Mkombozi* and his mercy, where would I be?"

"For one, I am glad I do not know," said Isoke, hugging Fola's arm in a rare display of emotion.

Lusala's eyes searched the horizon for her friend. She mistook quite a few men for him, as his stature, skin tone and musculature was common. He dressed like the others and assumed a normal gait. In short, nothing set him apart at a distance. In close proximity, though, his light brown eyes exalted him above all others in her mind.

"Eat," Bimnono said, elbowing her daughter. "He will return in time."

"I am concerned, mother," Lusala said. "The Otī must have discovered him."

Muuaji examined Chimelu's face closely. *Kaizari was correct. Mkombozi lives after all.* If not for his spy, who said he witnessed the miracles performed firsthand just this morning, Muuaji may still wonder as to the identity of the Uché savior. The revelatory gestures inspired hope in the slave population; a hope he would now crush.

"Have you nothing to say before I slay you openly, now, in my court?"

Chimelu retreated inward and closed his eyes.

"So be it. Kill him."

The king's chief guardsman swung a sword at Chimelu's neck with all his might. Muuaji anticipated the moment where the blade would lop off his enemy's head and send it rolling, but the strike never connected. It was as if the guardsman never moved. He attacked Chimelu with an array of motions, but the sword did not penetrate. After exhausting himself, the soldier poked Chimelu with his index finger and felt solid flesh. The man did indeed exist, but he could not be harmed.

Muuaji left the throne, snatched the weapon from his guardsman, held it up to Chimelu's chest and slowly pushed the tip near the heart. When it made contact, but did not pierce the skin, he smiled. Muuaji cocked his elbow and forced the copper sword forward. Pain blasted through his hand, into his wrist and down his arm. Muuaji shouted and dropped the blade to the palace floor, where it snapped in two.

"Summon me my chief magician at once!" he yelled to two of his courtiers, still gnashing his teeth. Moments later, they returned with several dark magicians instead, as Zarek was nowhere to be found. "Will my chief magician not be found?"

"We are well able to accomplish your desires," said one. "How should you like him to die, your majesty?"

The king stroked his beard. Chimelu had embarrassed him in front of the royal court, proving impervious to attack. He wanted the infidel to suffer, but also wished an end to this conflict and a fulfillment to the prophecy of his victory. "He is to be the last cleric to wield unnatural abilities. In that manner, he should die unnaturally. I wish to look upon his bones and trample on his ashes."

All the magicians mumbled a chant in unison. A swarm of locusts materialized at the palace's great window. Muuaji laughed, as they commanded the insects to eat the flesh of their adversary, but the riotous horde surrounded the magicians instead and quickly consumed them down to the bone. When the skeletons touched the palace floor, they burst into flames and continued burning until only ash remained. Afraid for their lives, the palace courtiers dashed from the king's presence, all but two.

Moved by the display, Muuaji ordered the Uché slave back to the yam plantation. The remaining two courtiers, Uché brothers named Odion and Ochen, escorted him – after first entreating him not to deal with them the same way he had dealt with the magicians. After all, they only followed the orders of the king and did not necessarily agree with them.

"If you do not believe in the commands of your king, then choose a new king," he said at the palace gates. "One in whom you can believe."

They looked at one another. *Did the Uché cleric suggest that we overthrow Muuaji?* "If we leave the service of the king, who will provide protection for us?" asked Odion, the eldest. "Who will keep us from his coming wrath? You may be a cleric, and know *Njia*, but you are still a *slave*."

"Then you have chosen."

"He has performed wonders before us," argued Ochen. "He withstood the might of a sword and the black death of the locust. Could he not choose to protect us, as well?"

"Is it within your will, cleric? Will you do what your people believe you will do?"

"Follow me," Chimelu responded. "Leave your master and find out."

As Odion, Ochen and Chimelu continued this discussion while approaching the fields, Lusala caught sight of them and joy sprung from within her heart, for she knew it was *him*. She signaled Bimnono, who responded by waving to Isoke. She smiled.

"*Tazama Mkombozi,*" Isoke whispered to herself.

# FIFTEEN

## THE FIRST DAY OF FEASTING PRIOR TO FLOOD SEASON, 18 YEARS INTO ENSLAVEMENT, 21 A.B.

After Fola's healing and the raising of the dead soldiers, interest in *Njia* among the Uché experienced a renaissance. Following supper each night, Chimelu eschewed resting to share lessons about the mysterious power that Auni taught him to control and what he learned about it on his own. He spoke with wisdom and maturity far beyond that of his peers, as if he had lived *lives* prior to this one that they shared; so much so that the older men still believed he was Auni, Mosi, or one of Mosi's eleven brothers resurrected.

To learn *Nija*, on even a rudimentary level, he claimed that one had to embrace the belief that *all things* were possible, and anyone – Uché. Sanguë, or even Otī – could learn it. It had been previously taught that only those of Uché blood could master it, but Chimelu dismissed it as a falsehood spread by those wishing to keep its secrets exclusive. Only a small remnant, mostly young men of fighting age and women of similar age accepted this concept easily and without protest. The others, hardened by captivity and 18 years in slavery, rejected the idea. Above all the others, it was this assertion that thinned out the crowd the most.

But it did not deter Lusala. Though a quarter-blooded Otī, she ascribed to this belief. Based on this burgeoning maturity, Bimnono asked her husband to postpone Lusala's marriage arrangement, but he had already found a suitor and would give the maiden away on the final day of feasting. The marriage would likely end any devotion she found for EL, as the Sanguë worshipped many gods, and her husband would not tolerate EL's inflexible requirement to be preeminent.

But Isoke still struggled to believe, privately confiding in her son that she doubted. Chimelu admonished her, claiming that, if nothing else, she should believe all things were possible because of the miracles she had seen. Auni said something similar to her long ago, but the encouragement inspired more questions than answers. *If all things are possible through Njia, it means that for 800 years, the Uché have been captives only because they had the key to free themselves and shunned it.* She could not accept that as truth.

At a gathering the first night of feasting, those Uché and Sanguë committed to hearing Chimclu huddled around a fire and shared kola nuts. With Lusala and Isoke to his right, Fola and Letsego to his left, he repeated the need for the Uché to abandon their tendency to waver between exclusive worship of EL and other gods, and the limitations dominating their minds. Letsego appointed himself Chimelu's opposition that night, audibly challenging him face-to-face on the authority by which he spoke.

"Am I; are we, to believe what you say, as you are barely of fighting age?" Letsego's rhetoric evoked sounds of agreement from his peers. "We have seen many battles, Chimelu, and lost loves dear to our hearts! And you say to us, that through *Njia*, we could have thrown off our shackles at any time? Unbelievable!"

Isoke watched closely for Chimelu's reactions. His nostrils did not flare, nor did his eyes narrow, as they had done during previous confrontations. Chimelu rubbed his hands, but did not clench him. *This time,* she thought, *they have not gotten to him.*

"Why do you do not believe that the power I have is inherent within all of you?"

"Because you are *Mkombozi*! According to the prophecies, you are supposed to free us, not *ourselves*. Yet, you have been among us for almost a year and we still labor beneath the thumbs of our oppressors. Why should we believe in that power; just because you raised a few men from the dead? Why should we believe in *you?*"

Letsego stirred up latent anger and frustration within the crowd. *Why has he not freed us yet? Is he waiting for more of us to die? Or is he a dark magician in disguise, sent by the Otī?* It had long been rumored that a spy labored among them, but no suspects were ever success-fully identified. The crowd formed a mob around Isoke, Fola, Lusala, and Chimelu, who led them away from the fire to a loud roar.

"See, he is not *Mkombozi!*" Letsego yelled. "*Njia* is dead. Go back to your homes. If we are to be freed, it will be by our own mortal hands, not by his!"

As Chimelu tunneled away through the masses, Lusala caught him by the wrist and stopped him. "Go back and face them," she encouraged. "They could not discern the truth if it slapped them in the face. Make them see in you what I see in you."

To many jeers, Chimelu stormed back to the fire. Prior to his death, Auni warned him to never allow pride or a desire to be honored by influencing his decisions. But while pride and honor were at stake, the name of EL was also on the line, as Letsego declared *Njia* to be dead. The Uché cleared a path back to the fire where Letsego, convinced that he had triumphed, faced Chimelu and crossed his arms. "Have you returned," he asked snidely, "to convince us without *truly* convincing us, *Son of Mosi?* If you were truly *Mkombozi*, we would not labor another day for the Otī. You would go to the Revelation Gate and end this."

At that, Chimelu retreated again, with Lusala following close behind. Isoke turned to Fola, who indicated that she should let Lusala comfort him for now.

Chimelu opened the door to his hut and expressed his frustrations through punching the clay wall. At any moment, he could have killed Letsego in a variety of unnatural ways for questioning him, and then raised him back to life. He could have called fire or pestilence from the skies to strike down his doubters, or even petitioned Mlinzi to cut them down as he had done to the overseer in the field. But, if they were to believe in him as *Mkombozi*, he could not influence their wills that way. According to Auni, EL's enemy Zarek and his minions operated through fear, and did so effectively, but followers of *Njia* were forbidden to do so.

Lusala entered the dimly-lit hut and found Chimelu starting a fire at the hearth for warmth. The hour was late and his housemates would not return until the celebrating had concluded. They were alone and would be for some time.

"Be eased," she said, wrapping her arms around his shoulders.

"How can I be?" He eased from her touch. "My own people reject me."

"Did they not reject EL *first*? It seems logical, then, that they would reject the Son of EL."

Chimelu exhaled and fiddled silently with the fire's unlit kindling. For the first time, Lusala noticed the symbol hanging around his neck, as it was exposed.

"What is that around your neck?"

Self-conscious, he pulled his clothes over it. "Nothing."

"We have known one another closely, Chimelu. There is something you cannot share with me, though I believe in *Njia*?"

Chimelu pondered telling her about the Revelation Gate. It was a burden he carried alone since the start of the last harvest and wished to share it, but he did not feel the timing was right. "Auni gave it to me," he admitted. "Sometimes, it is all I feel I have left of him."

"I was of the understanding that the souls of the dead travel to the next realm. If this happened to him and will also happen to you, will you not see him again?"

"I will." A tear rolled down his cheek. "I miss him, though . . .his guidance."

Lusala embraced Chimelu and held him close to her bosom. He hesitated to return it, but placed his hands on her upper back. As he pulled away from her, Lusala closed her eyes and moved closer for a kiss. Chimelu turned his cheek to her inviting lips and backed away.

Embarrassed, Lusala wiped her mouth and composed herself. "I am to be given to another in a few days. I want to be with you and you alone. Can it be arranged so?"

Chimelu shook his head. "It cannot. We are forbidden to marry, by my vows and the Otī."

At that, Lusala slipped out of her clothes. "Then have me another way."

Chimelu had never seen a female nude before and everything Lusala presented was pleasing. If they made love, she would be unfit to marry. While Sanguë men were infamous for their licentious habits, brides were expected to be virgins on their wedding nights. Furthermore, while Uché law allowed a cleric to marry and have sons and daughters, according to Auni, the Son of EL was not permitted to do so.

Despite his inner desire to touch Lusala and to grant her what she requested, he left her naked and kneeling on the cold earthen floor.

## SIXTEEN

## THE LAST DAY OF FEASTING PRIOR TO FLOOD SEASON, 18 YEARS INTO ENSLAVEMENT, 21 A.B.

Humiliated, Lusala tearfully clutched the sheets close to her naked body, only to have them snatched away by the father of her intended husband.

"Whore!" The older man open-hand slapped her, sending her into hysterics. Her co-conspirator, a young Sanguë with whom she had been caught fooling around with before, had been excused from the scene of the crime. "I agreed to this union as a favor to your kin . . . because I *pitied you.* Aitan was a friend of mine and you have disgraced his name by committing this crime."

"I did not want him," she muttered. "Nobody asked for your pity."

Before he could strike her again, Bimnono's husband restrained him and escorted him outside, leaving Lusala and her mother alone. The girl continued crying miserably, and though Bimnono wished to strip the skin off of her body for this betrayal, she laid a comforting arm around her daughter. "I just do not understand why you would do such a thing. Aitan and I did not raise you to lift your dress to just anyone – despite what our culture allows. And you have had your troubles . . .we all have. But this? Have you nothing to say for yourself?"

"I did not love him, Mama," she sniffed. "I tried, but I could not."

"Love is a decision to have a feeling, not a feeling you cannot decide. You could not tell it by looking at me now because I am old and fat . . .but, I could *dance.* One day, your father saw me and I guarantee you that love was not the first thing on his mind. He took me as his second wife, and day after day, we *decided* to love each other. It is our custom to do such things."

"But what if. . .I decided to love . . . have feelings for . . . someone else already?"

"*That boy* who just dragged himself out of here? You have already had the marriage night; it would be difficult, but not impossible."

"No, Mama." Red-eyed, Lusala wiped her cheeks dry with her hands. "He is magnificent and of valor. He is strong and determined. He always does the right thing, no matter what it costs him. His reputation is up-standing. There is no other. *He* is the man I desire to join in marriage."

"Who is this you speak of?" she wondered aloud, before realization struck her. She wanted the one person that she could not have. "Young one, you *think* that you love him. But, you do not. It is the tenderness of caring that you feel, or fondness."

"No, Mama." There was resolve in Lusala's statement. "I have felt those things for others before. This is . . . *different.* And I am no fool. I know he has taken vows and does not . . . cannot express the same feelings toward me. The other night, I offered myself to him and he spurned me. I *am* a fool!"

Bimnono gathered Lusala's clothing from the floor and tossed it onto the makeshift bed. "Get dressed. You cannot sob here forever."

Lusala obeyed orders. "What is to become of me now?"

"You get dressed," said Bimnono. "Walk out of this hut with as much dignity and pride as the boy who left you here to face judgment. You decide to stop loving Chimelu, close your legs and live a quiet life. Eat supper, go to sleep, rise tomorrow and decide to stop loving Chimelu . . . close your legs and live a quiet life."

The next morning, the first of the flood season, Lusala awoke in her hut to staring, pointing and whispers from her housemates. She did not have to imagine what they talked about, because her affair was the talk amongst all the female slaves. Those who lost their maidenhood by being parceled out as chattel to the men garnered compassion, while giving their virginity away independently was *detestful*. Now, no man would want her – except to serve in the station of a similar capacity. She would be considered ideal for that.

*So, I will never be married,* she thought on the way to Bimnono's hut after breakfast. *I do not want to wed any man unless it is Chimelu. Even if he never touches me, if he looks at me in his way, it would be enough. Mama does not understand. No one understands. If I cannot have him, then I desire none at all.*

Bimnono greeted her daughter with a quick hug and a bowl of porridge. Lusala ate out of courtesy, for the last vestiges of her hunger still knelt on Chimelu's floor. "Where is he?" she asked, referring to Bimnono's husband.

"Outside the gate with a pipe. You did not see him? You must have just missed one another."

Lusala dawdled tracks in the cereal's surface with her spoon. "Must have."

"Have you decided for today?"

"I have decided not to act again, but I cannot decide not to love him. Be sure, I will not act upon it again, but if I do not act on it – it is not because I do not feel it."

Satisfied for the moment, the two ate in silence. Afterward, they joined the procession to the work camps, engaging in idle conversation so the gossips, the intrigued, the curious, and the titillated would not pester them with intrusive questions. At the work site, however, she did not have the patience to ignore the constant inquiries.

One of the girls, still a maiden and unconsidered by the Otī to pair off for mating, scooted over next to Lusala. "So, how was it? Good, bad, in between?"

Instead of the uninteresting truth, Lusala decided to lie. "I will tell you, but only you because I can trust you. Do not tell another soul! Swear it on your life."

"I swear!" she eagerly agreed. "On my life, I swear."

"Look at that animal over there," she said, pointing toward a male calf. "Not quite that big, but comparable. I screamed like none have ever screamed before."

The girl's eyes widened, as she had no experience with which to refute Lusala's claim. "And *that* is how you got caught?"

"Mmmhmm." Lusala bit her lip to stifle the laughter. "Could not control myself."

At the time to break for meal time, the girl in whom Lusala confided shot off to tell her friends, who fell down to the ground in laughter. Lusala smiled at the scene and joined Bimnono at the great stump.

"Mischievous imp!" She elbowed her daughter. "What have you done?"

"I gave one of them a little something to talk about."

"You have given them enough," she warned. "Take care before it becomes your ruin!"

As the overseers had taken turns celebrating the five days of feasting, rest for the Uché lasted longer than normal. Lusala seized the opportunity to talk to Chimelu, who now spoke to a smaller group whose faith in him had not completely failed. Upon seeing the girl, whose reputation stood just a bit better than a woman of ill repute at this point, the people excused themselves and drifted away.

"There is something that you should know, Chimelu," she said. "I have feelings for you and you have taken vows against returning them, but I feel them still."

He held her hand within his and concentrated on Lusala's quivering lips.

"I will not act on them again; you have my word," she affirmed. "But also know that I will always love you. I will *never* stop loving you. And, if you would ever change your mind about us being together, I will be yours forever."

Chimelu clenched his hand around hers until she pulled it away and departed. He did have affection for his friend, even sparks of attraction, but he could not admit it. Confessing them openly would controvert the vows he had sworn before Auni: to forsake romantic relationships and focus on loving collectively. Like Lusala, he had feelings to suppress and not to cultivate. He appreciated her friendship and support and hoped not to lose either. He would need them for the times to come.

Near sundown, Chimelu met Fola and Isoke, as Bimnono and Lusala walked on their own away from the trio. Since the confrontation with Letsego four nights ago, Isoke and Fola harbored rising doubts and a loss of respect for Chimelu. He labored among them since the last harvest, and now another rainy season was upon them. *What was he waiting for? Why has he not gone to the Revelation Gate yet?*

They did not brusquely broach the subject, as Letsego had done, but wondered nonetheless. Fola argued that, as his mother, Isoke should ask. He would not likely deny her. But, she countered, Fola was a man of military knowledge and would be able to advise Chimelu on mobilizing and commanding the Uché against the enemy – he should ask. Unable to come to a conclusion, they cast lots and the lot fell to Fola.

"Chimelu," he said, as they neared the encampments. "When you prepare to venture to the ends of the realm, be assured that our resources will be yours to command. It shall be done as you say, as soon as you need it."

"Thank you." He said nothing else.

"Will you be going *soon*? If I know, I can prepare the men accordingly."

"We live in houses of mud, but the House of EL is in *ashes*. The temple has been destroyed and must stand again."

Incredulous, Isoke jumped into the conversation. "We labor from sunrise to sunset. Whose back will be broken in order to rebuild it?"

"Tomorrow, I will have an audience with the king and he will not refuse me this."

Late that same night, after sleeping with Penda and dismissing her, Muuaji could not find rest. He tucked the translation of the Uché prophecies underneath his arm and ascended to the roof of the palace, where reading in the night air would fatigue him. There, beneath the torchlight, he spread the scroll over a table and read.

*He is the Son of Mosi and will dwell amongst them. His name is Chimelu,* Muuaji discovered, which means *made of our god* in the Uché language. *He dwelled in the slave encampment.*

*They will mock and accuse him, and he will do the unnatural in their midst.* He remembered the ways Chimelu defied death in the throne room, by the sword, the host of locusts and bursts of fire.

*His bones cannot be broken,* Muuaji pondered. *The fall in the well did not kill or break him.* He read on. *They will hear his words, but not believe them. He will worship in the dwelling of EL, and mete justice to all.*

He paused to consider what *the dwelling of EL* was . . . *the temple?* He had ordered its destruction before enslaving the Uché almost 20 years ago. *Will the Uché attempt to construct a place of worship once more?*

According to Kaizari, each of the prophecies must be fulfilled prior starting the war, *Mkombozi's* journey to the Revelation Gate, and his death at Muuaji's hands – not before. Therefore, should the Uché attempt to build another temple, he could not refuse them, though it may take years to properly do so.

Early the next day, prior to the sun's rising, a courtier entered the king's chambers. As Muuaji slept lightly as to avoid attempts on his life, he immediately became aware of the servant's presence. "Why do you disturb my slumber, Ochen?"

He bowed in obeisance. "The Uché slave Chimelu, of the house of Aitan, requests an audience with you, sire."

Muuaji massaged his weary eyes. "Zarek is still not to be found?"

"No, your majesty." Ochen draped a kingly robe over Muuaji. "Our men cannot find him. It is as if he never existed."

"Summon the magicians and assemble my guard in the throne room."

Once Muuaji composed himself and the party assembled, he assumed his seat at the throne and signaled with his scepter for Chimelu, now a man of fighting age, to come forward. He did so humbly, but did not bow before the throne. While the 20 soldiers and 15 magicians wondered whether or not the king would order him to kneel, they did not voice their thoughts, nor exchange furtive glances. The Uché slave could not be killed, but they could.

"You requested an audience with me. Speak."

"If it pleases the king," Chimelu said, gathering his courage. "I ask to grant me the land to rebuild EL's temple."

Inside, Muuaji leapt for joy over what a rebuilt temple meant. "The flooding of the District River starts. Even if I grant you land, nothing can be built successfully during the flood season."

"If I may be so bold, allow your servant to construct the foundation out of the harder substances of the earth, and upon that surface, EL's temple will stand again."

"And who shall retrieve it from the ground? Your people work their hands at my ploughs from the sun rising to its setting."

"I am a cleric, like Auni before me," he claimed. "If it pleases the king, afford me the same labor-free privilege that you granted him."

Muuaji stroked his beard. From the field reports, Chimelu had but few followers. "You will need others to aid you. Choose as many men as are willing."

Chimelu nodded in agreement. "You have spoken well. Let it be unto your servant, as you have said."

# PART THREE

# SEVENTEEN

## THE FIRST DAY OF FEASTING BEFORE FLOOD SEASON, 20 YEARS INTO ENSLAVEMENT, 23 A.B.

Since reconstruction of EL's temple commenced almost two years ago to the day, Letsego attempted to convince the populace to attack the Otī armaments again and again, but to no avail. Fola, his biggest opponent on military matters, gained a measure of standing with his people each time Letsego tried and failed. Each time, they forwarded a different excuse.

The Otī allowed the reconstruction of the temple, which meant religious freedom once again. The sudden relevance of *Njia* sparked interest in the Uché. *It is as if they await something.* Try as he might to suppress it, Letsego sensed enthusiasm rising with the setting of the cornerstone to the foundation and, just recently, the temple's completion. He did not understand why Muuaji allowed the structure to stand, but suspected sinister motives behind it.

The king gave them a choice location impervious to high water during flood season, the use of materials and a significant number of slaves to work exclusively on the temple a few days a week. The labor was equally as grueling as the backbreaking labor they were used to, but the end product benefitted them and thus, their attitudes improved. The labor songs turned from funeral dirges into joyous tunes which rang aloud from sunrise to sunset. What started with a few faithful evolved into a populous *movement* that Letsego refused to support.

"Trickery!" he would yell to anyone who listened. "How soon will EL's temple be built, lest the Otī change their minds and tear it down brick by brick? They have crushed our hopes before, burnt our belongings and beheaded our own. Yet, you believe they have suddenly reconciled themselves to us through this act of repentance? Are we not still slaves who die each day?"

Chimelu tried to quell the insurgents, prophesying that the temple of EL would stand *forever* and EL's honor preceded their freedom. Muuaji's palace, the oldest structure in the known realm, had existed no longer than 40 years. They scoffed at Chimelu's claims and spit at him, for if he was truly *Mkombozi*, he would have gone to the Revelation Gate long ago. Muuaji surely planned to destroy the temple, and Chimelu wasted their time and spent their hope. Gradually, as doubts mounted, support for the temple waned, leaving its completion to the cleric, less than a dozen men and a few Sanguë women.

Despite the now-completed temple, Letsego accomplished his mission. The people were discouraged and remained so. Muuaji would be pleased and may finally promote him.

Lusala worked closely with Chimelu, preparing as many of the temple's furniture as she was allowed. She did believe in *Njia*, which entitled her to inclusion in the process, but as she indulged in a lifestyle contrary to its tenets, Chimelu was forced to exclude her from preparing certain objects. She had no husband and was not marked to breed by the Otī, but freely slept with anyone who showed interest. She had been threatened by the former wives of the men, and struck or cut for it on occasion. Chimelu knew so by the random bruised eyes and facial gashes. But he said nothing. Lusala wished he would condemn, praise, criticize her, or just say *something*.

That afternoon, outside the building itself, the pair assembled the sacrificial altar alone, as Bimnono, Odion and Ochen searched for wood and an animal to slay.

"How do you stay encouraged, Chimelu?" Lusala blurted out. "Your people, even your mother and your kin, forsake you. They are bitter slaves. Yet, you have not shed one tear in sorrow."

"I ask EL each day for the strength to continue and to do what must be done. Look around you! Those who laughed at and cursed me thought that it could not be accomplished, yet here we are standing inside of the fulfillment of a promise. Two years ago, this land was barren and without form or foundation. If the Uché were all blind, this could have been built in half the time."

"*Blind?* I do not understand."

"The blind are not limited by what they see because they cannot see. If you tell a blind man, 'Beware! There is a pit ahead,' he will stop and not proceed. A sighted man will believe you if he can verify it himself, but will cease to move if he does not."

"I believe you," she said, somewhat sentimentally. "I always have." An awkward silence followed. Chimelu inadvertently touched Lusala's hand, while fitting the platform into the carved grooves of the sacrificial stone, sending her into a fit of tears.

He produced a cloth and gave it to her. "Be comforted, my friend."

"Comforted . . .by what?" she sniffed. "Will you finally love me? Will *someone?*"

Lusala's bed hopping reputation bothered him, so much so that he often refrained from food and meditated in an attempt to gain understanding. He felt the urge to be pleased sexually by her, but did not submit to his desires. Romantic love did bubble in his heart, but he stifled it. Chimelu kissed his fingertips and laid them on Lusala's lips. Lusala reciprocated, her fingers lingering on her lips before lovingly brushing them against his cheek. Fornication made her unclean, and, therefore, unavailable to have more than casual contact with a cleric.

Chimelu held her hand against his face. A tear dropped from his eye and dotted her fingertips. He knew she had crawled from the bed of another man before arriving to finish the temple, had slept with another man prior to that one, and plotted to consort with yet a different one after she departed from him. Chimelu wanted to satisfy the longing in her soul himself. But he could not do so alone.

"I have to go," said Lusala. She turned away and did not look back.

"We have returned!" Odion and Ochen announced. They had left their offices under Muuaji's permission and at Chimelu's specific request, brought a young calf and an armful of wood. "Bimnono has returned to the encampment. And we have been summoned and will report back to our stations tomorrow."

"So be it," said Chimelu. "I am to go before the king this evening to report our progress."

He arranged the wood within the stones first, secured the sacrifice upon the altar with binds at its legs and arms, and slit its throat. The animal struggled and gagged for a moment, then collapsed lifelessly as the flames rose to incinerate it. Chimelu bowed his head and demonstrated that Odion and Ochen follow suit. They silently remembered their offenses against EL at that time. While he had none of his own to confess, Chimelu thought of Lusala and pled forgiveness on her behalf.

Meanwhile, as Lusala removed her clothes, she thought of Chimelu with pride. *Despite the ridicule and lack of support, he did it. EL's temple stands again!*

"Make haste!" boomed an impatient voice. "My housemates will not tarry long."

Struck with a sense of conscience, Lusala reconsidered. "I will not," she said, gathering her dress.

The man cursed her and got up himself. "Are you now a whore with morals?"

She resisted the urge to strike his vulnerability. For the first time since the first time, Lusala held her head with esteem. By the time she returned to the temple, the sacrificial fire had been reduced to embers and the area was vacant. All that remained was a circle burnt into the altar's surface, with four lines intersecting a central line at two points.

Now that EL's temple had been rebuilt, Muuaji looked to Zarek for guidance. His chief magician reappeared, it seemed, only when the king was desperate for answers. His flightiness aggravated Muuaji, but the powerful magician could not be reasoned with, or forced to change his ways. Since the construction of the temple, though, he held an audience with the king quite regularly. He needed constant assurance that the temple indeed started the timeline toward *Mkombozi's* demise and would not result in his overthrow, as the Uché prophecies declared.

Before Chimelu reappeared before the throne at sundown, as he had commanded, he beckoned Zarek once more.

"What is your request, sire?" he asked.

"Show me the fate of my adversary once more, and the triumph of the Otī."

Zarek called for a golden bowl large enough to fit a small child. After sprinkling a dark powder onto its concave surface, he spat in it and flourished his hands. An explosion burst from inside the bowl, sending black smoke into the air. Billowing gray clouds rumbled in the explosion's aftermath.

"What do you see, Zarek?"

"See for yourself."

Muuaji leaned forth. Inside the sanctum of the finished temple was a fashioned wooden circle with four lines intersecting with a central line at two points. Then, Chimelu came into view – bloody, naked and viciously beaten. Finally, he and Kaizari drank new wine in celebration of their victory over the Uché savior. "What is that symbol, prophet? Do not deny me my request. Interpret what I have seen."

"You have looked into the future," said Zarek. "The symbol you have seen is the Revelation Gate of the Uché prophecies. The five lines represent five turns of the sun. At that time, the war will begin, and *Mkombozi* will enter it."

"And *I* am to permit this?" Angered, Muuaji rose from the throne. "I will send men to the temple and destroy this gate before he enters it."

"You must not," Zarek warned. "The Revelation Gate is our only hope of harming him. If he does enter it, he will lead the Uché to victory. Remember the final prophecy: his blood will run over your hands."

Muuaji pondered Zarek's statement. "You have spoken well," he said. "Tell the Uché cleric Chimelu that I bid him entrance."

Just as Chimelu entered, Zarek exited before the king noticed. He held out his scepter, clearing Chimelu to approach the throne.

"It has been done, as you requested," Chimelu said. "The temple is complete and any who aided me will report to their stations at the rising of the sun. Now, as the flood season approaches, I am to enter the inner sanctum and make sacrifice for my people. I will not appear before any man until it is complete."

"How many turns of the sun until the flood?" Muuaji asked him.

"Five."

Muuaji restrained his pleasure. "And how long until your sacrifice is complete?"

"Whatever EL demands," he responded. "It could be days, or moons, or a season may pass before I reemerge."

"Let it be according to your words!" Muuaji proclaimed.

At dinnertime, Odion and Ochen joined Bimnono and Lusala, Isoke and Fola, and Letsego. Though they ate at separate tables, the seven interacted regularly and enjoyed communing with one another. Chimelu entered, shook the dust from his sandals, and washed his hands and feet before joining them. Isoke prepared his portions and set them before him. Lusala looked in his direction, eager to confide in him of her triumph. Chimelu gave thanks and ate ravenously. It reminded Isoke of how he had eaten the first time they met as adults.

"You must see the temple, Mama," Chimelu said. "It is everything the temple of our ancestors must have been."

Isoke did not respond. She had not helped her son lift one stone during construction, and did not plan to worship or sacrifice there.

"It looks so from the distance," Fola interjected. "It is soon to flood, Chimelu. Is it not time for you to sacrifice on our behalf?"

"Yes . . .tomorrow morning at the sun's rising. You must begin preparations."

"Preparations?" He looked perplexed. "Preparations for what?"

"The war shall begin in five days."

All conversations at the table stopped at the mention of war. It was the moment the Uché people had anticipated for 823 years; the time where they would take up arms against their adversaries. Fola, now 54 and a grizzled, battle-tested warrior, stretched vigor into his limbs. "Finally!" he exclaimed. "We will battle united!"

"Wait!" Letsego yelled. "You will go to war on the word of a cleric who has not seen one day of battle, and will not even fight? He will be burning animals behind a veiled curtain! That is what you will be doing while we *die*, is it not?"

Chimelu controlled his anger. "I will go to the Revelation Gate."

The pronouncement temporarily silenced Letsego. *If he goes to the Revelation Gate, he knows what it is and where it is. I must find out as well.*

Isoke remembered the symbol burned into Hawa's palm. "Tell us of the Revelation Gate."

Chimelu removed the necklace Auni had given him. "This is what it looks like." He handed it to his left, first to

Letsego, who passed it to Ochen. Ochen reluctantly passed it to Odion, then to Bimnono, Lusala, and Isoke, who clutched it tightly. "It represents our success. In five days, once I enter, the war will end in our favor."

Letsego broke the silence. "Then tell us where it is, so that we may find it."

"It is not for you to find," said Isoke, echoing Hawa's words. "It is only for him – and those intending to take him to it."

"Who told you that, dear Isoke?"

"Hawa."

"*Hawa*?" Letsego scoffed. "That crazed. . ."

Fola snatched Letsego by the tunic. "Easy talking about the dead."

"You will enter it," posed Lusala. "But will you *exit* it, as well?"

Chimelu did not answer her directly. "The answers are coming, dear one."

After dinner, Lusala and Isoke escorted Chimelu to the temple, as he would now dwell there instead of the encampments. In another two watches, he would not be seen until after the seasonal sacrifice. The trio loitered at the gates for a time and then Lusala dismissed herself. She had said her peace and Isoke must do the same.

"What else did Hawa say to you, Mama?"

"She said. . .that I would see you enter the Revelation Gate."

Chimelu opened the wooden gate to the temple and entered the torch-lit courtyard. Isoke followed.

"You never gave an answer to Lusala. After you enter the Revelation Gate and the war is over, we will no longer see you, will we?"

"You will have to look in another place."

"You are a cleric, but you are also *my son*. Speak clearly to me and do not treat me like a child."

"In the coming days, you will be bound and shackled; you and the others," he admitted. Those who believed will not believe. Many Uché, Sanguë and Otī will die, but all these things must happen if we are to succeed."

Isoke shuddered. She buried her head into his chest. "Is there no other way?"

Knowing she asked EL and not him, he comforted Isoke as she wept over the future.

# EIGHTEEN

## THE FIRST DAY OF FEASTING BEFORE FLOOD SEASON, 20 YEARS INTO ENSLAVEMENT, 23 A.B.

Penda, now 49 years old, no longer held appeal for Muuaji and would die the next time he purged the harem. Sifa, who the king slept with the night after her husband Kabal's death four years ago, assumed the title of the favored concubine. Though, unlike Penda, she endured regular menstrual periods, Sifa's body was more supple and firm at the pleasurable points. The replacement was expected, occurring shortly after Penda offended him while trying to describe *Njia* to a foreigner.

Because concubines were privy to the inner workings of the kingdom and that of the king, Muuaji felt obligated to destroy them once he used them for all they were worth. He did so gruesomely in front of his current court to send a message that he was not to be trifled with. Penda had seen scores of women die during her time of service, and it did nothing to frighten her, but much to disgust her. The king's laughter echoed behind the backdrop of screaming agony and pleas for mercy.

Though Muuaji's attention diverted elsewhere lately, Penda intended to escape and hide amongst her own people. She helped to rescue Chimelu and, in doing so, thought Isoke may look upon her kindly. For days prior, she feigned ill while allowing her body to abstain from the Otī's thorough skin treatments. When her eunuch discovered her bare-faced, he alerted the king and forced her to confront him.

"Penda, what is the meaning of this insolence?"

"I know that you, oh king, dispose of the concubines who have displeased you, or lost their beauty at the hands of time." She licked her naked lips. "I ask you to remember the 27 years I served your father, and then you, and implore you to let me go down to my people rather than die miserably at your hands."

Impressed by her bravado, Muuaji raised his scepter. With the war to begin, Penda would soon perish regardless. "Leave my presence and do not return."

She curtsied and hurried from the palace before the king could change his mind. En route to the female slave encampment, she let her hair loose and broke into a joyous run. No longer was she Penda, the slave masquerading as a sexual plaything for the Otī, but Mairi, mother of Madiha, Sakina, and Gamba and sister to Isoke. This year, Madiha would turn 34 and Sakina 32. Gamba, her son, would have been 29. And dear, stubborn Isoke would see 50. She would celebrate with them, as the days of feasting had commenced, and join the stoutest of them in the fields or offer her breasts as a wet nurse. No longer would she lie on her back and commit death.

Mairi knocked door to door in search of Isoke until she came upon Bimnono, who told her where to find her.

"Isoke," she said out-of-breath. "I am no longer Muuaji's concubine!"

"Good for you," she said with disdain. "Should Fola give you a hero's reward?"

"I do not understand it. I bid him to allow me to come here, and he did so without remorse or reservation."

"He did so because we declare war in four days. Your blood will be shed, whether he does so, or not. It does not matter to him, nor does it differ to me."

Mairi ignored the bitter sharpness in Isoke's tone. "War?"

"We soon take up arms against the Otī for our freedom."

"Where are my children? Do my daughters live?"

Isoke's stance softened. "Sakina and Madiha both were marked for breeding and traded away for weapons. Whether they survived or not, I do not know."

Mairi muttered words in lament. "And *your* son?"

Isoke paused, unsure of what to reveal. "He is an empowered cleric now, and dwells inside the restored temple."

"Then if my blood is to be shed, I will not be idle. The king does not know so, but I am aware of his plans and the strategy of the Otī against you. . .us."

Isoke called for Fola, whose haste drew the attention of Letsego. As Mairi retold her announcement, Fola's ears perked. "Tell us then, of how they plan to attack."

On a map, Mairi used three-sided figures to represent the Otī squadrons. According to her diagram, they intended to occupy all the high places in the region. From there, Fola reasoned, the Otī could decimate the Uché troops through aerial attacks rather than hand-to-hand combat. As it stood, he would have to arm every able-bodied man and willing woman and send them into battle, though there was no effective counter to occupied high places that would not result in increased bloodshed.

Fola slammed his fist into the table. "This is disastrous, even worse than them trading us away. At least then we stood a chance at living!"

"Wait, brother!" Isoke pointed out several destinations. "Will they not have to *march* to reach these points? Can we station small attack groups in their path, hinder their progress and then filter our legions on those places under the cover of night?"

"Dear Isoke," he said with condescension. "What you propose is wise, but who is to know when they make their approach?"

"They do not," Mairi interrupted. "Muuaji shall not assemble until the third day."

"No king, even one as cowardly as he, discusses battle plans in front of a *woman*. . .particularly a foreign concubine. He must have meant for you to hear him, and plots to do otherwise."

"Fola," Mairi warned, "did you not learn from last time? I was a concubine, but his *most trusted concubine* whose ears he gave an audience on many occasions."

The reference to Chimelu's rescue brought a smile to Isoke's face. Even if it was a trap, the Uché had nothing left to lose. "Let us mobilize, brother, for time is short."

"And what if *he* is right, Isoke?" asked Letsego. "Whose son or father will you send as a sacrifice, while yours is under protection from EL inside the temple?"

"It is a *war*, Letsego. Sons and fathers will die, whether we set ourselves up or not; *how many* will be determined by our actions in the matter. We must not delay!"

"Then Fola," he said, continuing to plead his case. "You are a man of war and have seen many battles. Surely, you believe that this is a bad strategy! Will you wager the fates of our people on the word of the king's most trusted *whore*?"

Mairi slapped Letsego, whose attempt to reciprocate was thwarted by Fola. "See if you call me a whore again and have the lips to pronounce it a third time!"

"We will mobilize, Letsego, on *my* word." Fola sent a messenger to the militia's leaders to uncover the confiscated weapons and arm their legions for battle, but to await instructions.

Letsego nervously followed Fola and Isoke back to his hut. As a trusted member of the militia, he would be given orders and not have time to steal away to the palace to betray their confidence again.

"We will lose men, Letsego, even if we intercept them early," Isoke admitted, solemnly. Fola did not have to respond, and she knew it was true. "Do we even have a *chance*, brother?"

"Who knows how many of us there are, and who knows how many of them exist? We are undermanned and outarmed. Chimelu will enter the Revelation Gate in four days. His fulfillment of the prophecies is our one hope of turning the tide."

"Have faith in what we can control," said Isoke. "Whatever Chimelu does to help us will be a benefit, but we cannot idly sit by and wait for him. Our people have done so for 800 years to no avail."

"Then let me go to the palace," Letsego said with impatience. "I have found favor with the king in the past, and . . ."

"Are you crazed, Letsego? *No one* goes to the palace. He is more liable to kill you while he is drunk than sober. No, you will stay here with me."

Fola employed Letsego and Isoke as messengers throughout the day; him for the soldiers and her to encourage the women she thought able to pass for soldiers. What they lacked in upper body power, they more than made up for with guile. After one errand, though, Letsego neglected to report back. *That fool has gone to the palace and gotten himself impaled,* Fola thought.

When Letsego disturbed Muuaji's feasting by requesting an audience with him, the royal guard sharpened and posted a free pole in the garden. The king did not tolerate interlopers to his merriment – and a *slave* would incur his well-documented wrath.

Still fairly sober, the king shocked his courtiers by allowing the Uché slave into his presence four days shy of a now widely-known and anticipated conflict. Letsego knelt before the throne. "Oh great king, live forever!"

Muuaji sighed. "Yes, what is it now, Letsego? You have served me well, betraying your own brother unto death and sabotaging raids on my armaments. That and that alone is what now keeps your head on your body. Speak and make haste, and do not make mention of a reward to me."

Muuaji reneged on his promise to crown Letsego with glory and riches long ago, assuming the Uché throne for himself instead of appointing Letsego, or anyone else as successor. He shut his mouth and stuck to the matter at hand. "The Uché plot to occupy the high ground before you, even this very night," he said, still kneeling.

Muuaji stood. "Then let them have it. Is that all you have to report?"

"Chimelu will go to the Revelation Gate in four days."

He rose from the throne and nodded, looking behind Letsego. "It seems you, like your people, have outlived your usefulness to me, my friend. Do you have any information I can use?"

Letsego swallowed hard. *Fola was right.* "Spare my pitiful life! I have served as a spy for you, and your father before you. You know of *Mkombozi* because of me. I. . .I sent for him from the land of the Sanguë and slayed my only brother in your name. Surely, this is enough to save my life! Have mercy on me!"

En route to his dining hall, Muuaji paused at the stairs long enough to hear a *thump*.

Thinking that Chimelu would be serving in the inner sanctum and the other Uché concerned themselves with war matters, Lusala entered the temple's outer court to send a fragrant offering to EL. Her lips had not touched a man since Chimelu brushed them with his fingers. It was then that she believed *Mkombozi* was capable of doing more than raising the dead and moving objects with his mind. With one touch, he had removed the compulsive desire to do wrong. She only wished Chimelu had done so before her first experience and not her hundredth. Lusala remembered them all – by physical mark, voice, bodily scent, linguistic tendency or physical characteristic – like indelible, unique stains on her soul. He did not remove those memories, though she suspected that he could have done so.

The day's heat had passed its peak, but Lusala considered concealing her face with the hood of her outer cloak. Though her blood was more Uché than Otī, if others worshipped at the temple, she would be scorned and perhaps cast out because of her reputation. Instead, she donned a veil clear enough for her to see but not to be seen.

Odion and Ochen, who had become close to Chimelu, lingered in the courts near the sacrificial animal stalls. Both brothers saluted her, which she returned. They had spent enough time with Lusala to recognize her from a distance, but did not prevent her from sacrificing. *Who are we to interfere?*

Lusala prepared the offering, hoping to catch a glimpse of Chimelu. If he entered the inner sanctum, he would not be seen until after his service, which may very well be after the war commenced. Though the Otī king permitted its construction, if it presented a threat to him, or his preferences changed, he may destroy it out of spite. She may never see him alive again. If the prophecies were to be believed and they perished, EL would reunite them again in the next realm – if he did not send her to *Kuzimu*. But if she survived, she may live 60 years more!

Before the fragrance completely flickered out, Lusala gathered her dress in her hands and waited until the men were distracted to run up the uneven temple steps to the inner court of the temple. Without looking back, Lusala approached the curtain of the inner sanctum, as close as allowed, and knelt. Trembling, she reached a hand to the hanging fabric, careful not to touch it. She imagined Chimelu, a master of *Njia* and therefore aware of her presence, did the same thing on the other side.

*Speak to me*, she thought. *If you will, say a word to calm my aching soul.* She repeated the entreaty, closed her eyes, steadied her breathing and quieted her mind. Only then could she hear EL, or him if he spoke to her internally. The presence of another knelt to her right. She cracked an eyelid wide enough to determine the person's identity. By the type of clothing, she determined it to be a woman, also with a covered face.

Lusala stayed until her knees went numb and the sun moved beyond the trees. Her stomach rumbled with hunger and the urge to relieve herself pressed at her bladder. Still, she maintained a meditative state of mind. The faint, pungent scent of her fragrant offering wafted in the breeze flowing into the windows.

She pictured Chimelu stepping through the ceiling-to-floor curtain at the center. Wearing lightning-white garments and a sword hanging at his side, he invited Lusala to stand with him and proceed into the inner sanctum, which she did without hesitation. The place looked not unlike what she had imagined it to be – bare, except for an altar and a massive circular object fitted with four metal brackets hanging at two parallel spots at the top and two at the bottom. Inside the brackets were rusted metal spikes. Lusala stepped into the circle and, standing at the bottom, touched the bracketing. The meaning of it all impressed understanding upon her heart, and brought misery to it. She looked to Chimelu, who held a finger to her lips. She was not to reveal what she had seen.

Next to Lusala, Isoke assumed a similar posture. She estimated that the sun had moved at least two positions before her shoulders sagged and her mind ceased to flit from one thing to the other. Distractions proved to be her undoing. If she did not think of the battle, she thought of Fola and Letsego's rivalry, how long it had been since she had seen Sakina and Madiha alive, and exactly how her son labored behind the barrier. No one knew for sure, as sacrificing did not take a season to complete, but rumors persisted. *Whatever he does,* she thought, *my son is alive and not a slave.*

Odion and Ochen did not bother Isoke when she approached the temple. The mother of a cleric, if she lived, was permitted to see Chimelu at all times; except, of course, if he was sacrificing in the inner sanctum. She never admitted so openly, but missed her son and the brief moments they spent together upon his reemergence four years ago. She relished them with fondness – especially the times when he wolfed down her cooking, they playfully joked with one another, or he attempted to teach her the ways of *Njia* when it was clear that she had nothing but passing interest in them.

Gradually, her musings slowed to a stop. It was then that Chimelu parted the curtain for her. Behind it, she witnessed the view from a high cliff. She peered over the precipice and saw watered plains with abundant fruit and vegetation, trees and vibrant animals. The sun shone through waterfalls in the distance, creating bright prisms and rainbows reaching from crest to tributary. She surveyed the formally residential areas and found no people, but a scene worthy to be called paradise. The waste pits no longer existed, and the dreaded Valley of Bones had been emptied and closed over with earth. The meaning of it all was impressed upon her heart and brought Isoke to tears. She looked to Chimelu, who held a finger to her lips. She was not to reveal what she had seen.

Odion and Ochen lingered outside the temple's inner courts until first Lusala, then Isoke departed; each deeply affected by their time spent there. They locked the gates and carried long, curved, planks of wood stripped of their bark into the temple and stacked it outside the inner sanctum. They had done so for the past day, and tomorrow, would pound and shape four sets of iron shackles and poles according to the specifications Chimelu had provided them. For what reason, they did not yet know, but if the cleric trusted anyone, logic held that it would be them. By their reckoning, they did little to esteem themselves above the others who labored among them. But, at the laying of the temple's corner-stone, only the two plus Chimelu were present.

"Master," asked Odion at the time, after the cornerstone's setting. "Mosi's temple only stood for a few years. Shall this temple endure, or do we labor in vain?"

"Nothing you do today Odion," said Chimelu, "nor shall do for the next year is in vain. It shall remain as long as EL allows it to be, which is sufficient."

"Is sufficiency, in itself, enough?" argued the fiery Ochen. "Our people cannot lift eyes toward a symbol of hope and then watch it be snatched away again! Their belief in you must be rewarded."

Chimelu paused, for Ochen unknowingly spoke with a gift of foreknowledge. "They will lift eyes toward a symbol of hope and it will be desecrated in their sight. But they must have faith in order for it to be rewarded. Watch that they do."

## NINETEEN

## THE FIFTH DAY OF FEASTING PRIOR TO THE FLOOD SEASON, 20 YEARS INTO ENSLAVEMENT, 23 A.B.

With the District River already swelled to capacity, Muuaji thought it prudent to summon Kaizari and his troops before flooding commenced and made travel along traditional routes difficult. He appeared the morning of the fifth day, without ceremony or apology for arriving on the eve of battle. Muuaji had a throne customized for the larger man and set his own to its right. He bowed before the ruler, who extended a heavily-jeweled hand for his regent to kiss.

"Your throne, Kaizari. Notice the care with which it was constructed."

"Yes," he chuckled. "Care, indeed."

"My legions await your orders, sire. They are armed and at your command."

"Has your enemy landed blows?"

Muuaji recoiled. "They have secured some of the high places, yes."

Curious, Kaizari inquired further. "How many?"

"All . . .of them."

"And *Mkombozi?* He labors in the temple, yes?"

Muuaji concurred. "He does so, as my chief magician has revealed. This is the last night. I am curious, my lord. When will we strike?"

"Patience, Kgosi. High ground, low ground. . .these things are trifles. My men will join yours in overruning the Uché and tonight, you will storm the temple and bring *Mkombozi* before me. I will try him and tomorrow, you will kill him before his people."

Fola thought that claiming the high came too easily. Not only had the Uché suffered minimal losses, but the Otī and Sanguë were readily slain. For two entire days, the men occupied the perches, picking off those who dared venture across their paths, and sending their armor and weapons to the Uché who possessed none. It was as if Muuaji mocked them, giving them false hope and courage in the face of a coming onslaught.

Back inside of his hut, he fingered the metal object hanging around his neck. Isoke wore Chimelu's, and he fashioned one himself as a good luck charm. Other Uché soldiers caught the spirit of their commander and wore one, and the women painted it as a mark on the doors of their homes. In a way, the circle and five lines inspired them, though they knew not what it meant. To Fola, it equaled a sense of *chance*. If the Revelation Gate meant anything to him, it was the possibility of victory.

When the sun fell, the Uché would attack, sending men stationed behind the Otī city to scale the walls. Those at the high places were to focus their energy on crippling the enemy from the front. The flanks could attack from the sides and cut off the trade routes to prevent reinforcements. Though these attacks had been planned, they moved only on Fola's command, as Letsego had been missing for days. Rumor had it that his blood cried Muuaji's name from the royal garden grounds.

"Brother!" Isoke handed him a bowl of yam porridge and chunks of cooked meat. "Eat your strength, for tomorrow, we war for our independence."

While chewing, Fola noticed Isoke's necklace was no longer visible. "What does the object around your neck mean to you, Isoke?"

Occupied with her own eating, Isoke ignored the question at first. She sucked a stringy piece of meat from between her teeth and rolled her eyes. "It is the first thing, the only tangible thing, that my son ever gave to me."

"What else?"

Isoke remembered the vision, but also Chimelu's warning not to share it. "I am not certain. Why do you ask? What does it mean to you?"

"The prophecies state that *Mkombozi* will restore right order after he enters the Revelation Gate. I have to believe that the clerics did not die in vain all those years ago to protect a system of beliefs that is not true."

"So, you have become a believer in *Njia?*"

"I suppose I have. . .in a way."

She said nothing more on the subject, and the two ate in silence.

After Isoke tidied up, she and Fola intended to leave for the hidden armory. Instead, as they departed, sacks of animal skins were thrown over their heads, and their hands and feet were bound with heavy metal shackles. They were thrown with force into what they assumed was a wooden cart and transported for a time, then lifted and dropped onto a hard floor. Their captors unmasked them. Fola and Isoke had been thrown into a prison, along with Bimnono, Lusala, Odion, and Ochen, who had been previously captured. Bimnono's left eye had been blackened and Lusala licked her bleeding lip. Odion and Ochen bore numerous cuts and deep bruises.

"They wanted you two," whispered Odion. "They inquired of us all. Though we said nothing, they knew where to find you. It appears they beat us just for leisure."

"Without my command," Fola lamented, "the men will not know to attack and the Otī will surely destroy our strongest."

"And the women and children!" Isoke shook her head. "Mercy on us all!"

"The cruelty of our oppressors is outstanding," said Ochen, who coughed up a clot of blood. "I doubt it has been seen since the days of Mosi. You will hear our jailers mock us and, if it pleases them, flog us for no other reason but amusement."

Isoke looked at Bimnono, who said nothing. It was the longest period of time in the years they had known one another that she did not hear her speak. "Will you not speak, dear Bimnono?"

"I have nothing to speak of," she said, slightly rattling her shackles. Of the women, she put up the most fight in being abducted. By using her girth as leverage, she managed to land several blows to her captors before being knocked down. She recognized her husband's voice, as he protested, fought and was silenced. Unnatural deaths of spouses, especially more than one, meant the gods had cursed Bimnono.

Lusala leaned on her mother's shoulder. "It is not the end, Mama. It is only the beginning – not of our suffering, but of our *triumph*."

"It is the end for me, young one," she replied. "I am past the years of childbearing and without husband. Our own people side with the Otī and at the sun's rising, they will annihilate us and your kin."

"No, Mama, it is not so! Chimelu showed it to me and he would not speak lies."

"You know not of what you speak, Lusala," Isoke replied, warning Lusala with a look not to speak more of what she had seen. Lusala rambled on and on about how Chimelu's appearance had changed; so much so that she mistook him for a *god*. No one else in the cell knew what to make of it and Isoke dismissed it. Thus, they sat mired in relative silence in the cramped cell.

Fola maneuvered enough to see outside of the window. The prison's proximity to the District River explained the water leeching into the middle of the space. No one dared to dip their aching feet in or to sip from it; there was no telling how long the pool had been there or what lingered in it beneath the surface. All wondered what Muuaji intended to do now. If he abducted and jailed them, the other commanders and militia leaders may have been captured, as well. After throwing the Uché into chaos and annihilating the entire race, he would make sport of them. Tales of his cruelty were rarely embellished and never exaggerated. His brand of torture was protracted but definite in its end result. He would show them death eye-to-eye and they would taste its bitter sting.

Fola had fought many battles and bore marks from each. However, the scar he cherished above the others none could see. Four years ago, a sword pierced his stomach. Had it not been for Chimelu, he would not be shackled and imprisoned now. *But I lived!* Fola's mind worked on an escape plan. The guards were drunk from palm wine, and stumbled about the makeshift prison. If he somehow happened to unshackle himself, he, along with the others, could overcome them. *But, how can we safely return to the encampments?*

He looked to Odion and Ochen, who interpreted the narrowing of his eyes as the hallmarks of intrigue. But the brothers, expert fishermen in their own rights before the enslavement and their subsequent employment as courtiers, knew a thing or two about *patience*. The fish swimming in the District River were temperamental, sometimes choosing one side of their vessel to be caught and not the other, or refusing the customary bait. To catch them, one must be flexible in mindset and attitude, while determined to continue at all costs until the efforts proved fruitful.

Odion, the eldest of the two, believed that if Fola employed them in using these skills, an escape might be possible. He leaned over to Ochen and exchanged quiet conversation with him until they were warned to remain silent or speak aloud. *If we do escape*, thought Odion, *he will die first at my hands.*

At midnight, Isoke suddenly reared forward. Pain shot through her womb, not unlike the one that felled her when Chimelu was to about to be born. And she wailed, louder, longer, and far more terribly than she had then. The Otī guards cursed and threatened her in their language, but it did not stop her. Fola and the others attempted to comfort her before the jailers' patience waned. When the agony subsided, Isoke's eyes flew open. She covered her mouth in realization.

Across the land at the temple, Muuaji ordered his men to force the gates to the temple open. They complied and threw the doors wide.

Against Kaizari's wishes, Muuaji took a full complement of men with him, armed and equipped for a battle and not to capture one person. With caution, they approached up the uneven steps and into the inner courts. Rather than pushing the heavy curtain aside, the king ordered the men to cut it instead. Behind it was an altar, and the large wooden object Muuaji had seen in the vision Zarek presented him, though it appeared unfinished. *Where were the five lines?* Instead, there were metal brackets at the top and bottom of the circle.

Chimelu appeared from behind them and attacked, quickly dispatching most of Muuaji's battalion one blow at a time. Those in the back allowed the others to fall before making their attempt. He dealt with them similarly and only seemed to struggle with the lone member of Kaizari's soldiers. After fighting past the midnight hour, he was subdued and bound at the hands and feet.

Upon seeing that he was now able to be harmed, the king balled up a fist and punched Chimelu with all his strength, nearly toppling him over. He did it again and again until both his fist and Chimelu's face were raw and bloodied. Kaizari's soldier awaited further orders. Muuaji looked at his fallen men, and then at the Revelation Gate. "How many men do you think are needed to carry that?"

"One of ours," he replied. "Four of yours. It could be rolled."

"Unbind him and make him carry it. If he is *Mkombozi*, savior and king of an entire race of people, he can shoulder the load himself."

Chimelu grunted, as the weight of the Revelation Gate

was lowered upon his shoulders. He remembered the boulder that must have weighed at least this much and focused his energies upon making it lighter. But his powers had abandoned him.

The distance from the temple to the Otī palace never seemed longer. Splinters from the unfinished wood stabbed into Chimelu's hands and back. His muscles ached to the point of tearing, ribs throbbed with pain, and blood mixed with sweat dropped from his face. Still, he resolved not to give the king the satisfaction of rendering the situation agonizing for him. The cool night air did a little to refresh him.

The refreshment was not to be long, as Muuaji had him drop the Revelation Gate at a specific location high above what would be a battlefield at sunup. Summarily bound once more, he was taken to the palace before Kaizari. At the throne, the soldier who bound him kicked the backs of Chimelu's knees, sending him to the ground in indescribable pain. Though he lay before the throne on his side, he had not bowed – not even by force. Muuaji pulled him upright and slapped him a few times, laughing each time.

"Do you know who I am, Son of EL?"

Chimelu spat blood onto the carpet. "An abomination."

Kaizari waved his index finger and the soldier struck Chimelu in the mouth. "I am Kaizari, master to this realm. I have waited more than 800 years for the moment to confront you eye-to-eye. Will you defend your father and overthrow me?"

Chimelu said nothing, but bravely absorbed the blows doled out. Kaizari stood before him and wiped away Chimelu's blood with a cloth tinged with a bitter, stinging salve. "No. He will not overthrow me, not at all. Take him away. Throw him into the new cistern of your choosing and set a man before it."

The plan was ill-conceived, for all of the freshly-dug cisterns held a fair degree of water. Chimelu was tossed into one of the deeper wells. He sunk beneath the stale surface at first, then stood and waded through it. Considering the accuracy of the Uché prophecies to this point, Kaizari commanded them to insert the cover lid, just in case *Mkombozi* could grace the skies and escape. Its sealing drowned Chimelu in complete darkness, as the secure stone lid had no fissure.

With the understanding that he must go to the Revelation Gate, Chimelu first needed to move the lid. Try and mentally strain as he might, he could not budge it. He pounded his fist into the moist mud and limestone wall. Such an unstable surface would give in handfuls if he dared climb it.

"Mlinzi!" he yelled with fervor. "Mlinzi, if you are to protect me, then deliver me now from this enemy. If I am your Lord, then help me now, I command it!" His voice boomed in the enclosed space, but the herald did not appear nor deliver him. Chimelu invoked the name until it wearied him.

"Auni." His desperate voice funneled to a regular level. "Come to me, Father, and aid me. . .I beg of you. Lift me from the depths of this despair and deliver me that I may go to my people and defend them with the sword. If I am to go to this Revelation Gate and ascend the skies, how can I to do so from the bottom of a cistern?" Chimelu thrashed his arms in the water. "Answer me, Father!"

As soon as Chimelu ceased to move, silence resumed. He heard the faint squeak of swimming vermin and hoped that they did not smell his bleeding cuts. After quieting himself further, he barely noticed the cold water, the rats brushing past him, or the pain ebbing throughout his body. Soon, he slept standing up.

Just before the dawn signaling the beginning of flood season, the Otī soldiers guarding him dropped a rope for Chimelu to climb. At about the halfway point, his strength failed him and the soldiers lifted him out, only to flog him prostrate onto the dirt. The orange morning sun greeted them, barely peeking over the dusty horizon.

*Brian L. Thompson*

After binding Chimelu, they tossed him onto a cart and led it to the Revelation Gate. It was where it had been dropped, though it laid flat on the ground. Muuaji and Kaizari were present, amid enough soldiers to subdue ten men. Chimelu dismounted and was unbound, but surrounded by many weapons.

"Strip him," Muuaji commanded.

They did as they were told. Chimelu's body was purpled with dried blood and lumpy bruises. A gash above his left eye made it droop and his lips were split in several places. He now struggled to breathe, as one of his broken ribs had recently punctured his right lung. Shivering naked, he was forced onto the newly-created support boards of the Revelation Gate, which formed two lines intersecting a central line at two points. Chimelu voluntarily made fists and turned his hands inward to fit inside the brackets.

Muuaji giddily seized the sharp metal poles to bolt Chimelu into place. He positioned one to strike in between the two arm bones at the wrist and pushed it through the skin and sinew. Gritting his teeth, Chimelu grunted. Muuaji watched the blood spurt from around the wound and placed his hands underneath the flow. Indeed, the prophecy had been fulfilled. *His blood ran over the hands of his enemies.*

Inside the prison, few slept, anticipating the sounds of war and the destruction of the Uché at the hands of the Otī and Sanguë. Bimnono snored on Lusala's shoulder, while Isoke rested on Fola's. The men stood watch, while the soldiers slept off their wine. Lusala playfully jostled her wrist inside the heavy metal handcuffs. Suddenly, it sprung open! Without drawing attention, she jiggled the other shackle and it also loosened. Curious, she moved her legs to find out that those binds had already been broken.

Fola noticed this out of the corner of his eye and he

– 196 –

also found himself free. Putting his finger to his lips, he freed Isoke, Lusala freed Bimnono and the brothers loosened their own bonds. Before anyone could stop her, Lusala approached the door and pushed it open. Odion and Ochen rushed behind the girl and killed the guards, Odion specifically to the one he marked. The men armed themselves and placed the women at the rear. The sextet snuck out of the jail and into the open of the abandoned Otī compound. There, Fola passed a weapon and shield to each of the women.

"We must split up," reasoned Isoke. "The cause of our people is more important than our lives. You must get to the men and command them, brother."

Fola kissed Isoke and embraced her. "Be well and I will see you, if the sun chooses to wake." He, Odion and Ochen left through the gate and disappeared.

Bimnono looked at Isoke, with her good eye. "What are we to do now?"

Isoke clutched the shield in her hand. "We must go to see my son."

Frustrated by Chimelu's refusal to scream out in pain, Muuaji inserted the next pole violently, but to no greater effect. Conversely, he beat the remaining poles through the tissue in Chimelu's feet so slowly that Kaizari almost seized the instruments and did it himself. Finished and duly pleased, the king ordered it upon its stand. Six of his subordinates did so, placing the Revelation Gate on a weighted platform with two stumps to fit in the holes drilled at the bottom of the torture device. Presently constructed, it overlooked the battlefield perfectly.

"Had your people known what the Revelation Gate was from the start, do you think that they would have placed such abundant faith in it?" Muuaji clapped his bloodstained hands in mock praise. "Once Zarek showed me its true nature, I determined I should not see my last breath before seeing you enter it, and permitting your people to watch you die while I slaughter them at my hands."

Chimelu groaned, as he shifted his legs and arms to compensate for his collapsed lung. The nerve endings in his wrists and feet were on fire, though the rest of his body shuddered from exposure to the weather. Muuaji dismissed all but two of his soldiers to guard Chimelu, and those remaining behind tore his clothes to shreds and tossed them into the valley. Kaizari commended his regent, and the two of them rode off to the battle.

Isoke waited until the king and his troops exited the scene before she, Bimnono, and Lusala made an approach from behind the Revelation Gate. It was the elevated plain from her vision. The closer the trio approached, the more her stomach dropped. Lusala clutched hers and burst into hysterical tears that Bimnono forced her to muffle. She, too, cried for Chimelu. From the rear of the Revelation Gate, they could distinguish little but his entrapment inside it and sounds of agony.

Isoke dropped her shield and weapon, holding her hands up in surrender. Bimnono and Lusala followed suit. "We come in peace," said Isoke. "Do with us, your servants, as you will."

Lusala thought the men might abuse them, but they did not – only instructing them to stay quiet and not to attempt to free Chimelu. She rounded him first, covering her mouth in shame for him, and wept. Bimnono supported Isoke, who nearly fell faint.

"Mama." Unable to cover himself, Chimelu hung his head.

Isoke did not speak. Her son knew her heart. The horror of the scene brought sadness. Though she anticipated the worst possible, Isoke did not imagine *this*. She knelt beside his punctured right foot and rocked back and forth. Lusala did the same on his left. Bimnono stood adjacent to the men. *They must allow them to mourn.*

Fola, Odion and Ochen returned without incident and sooner than they imagined. Several hours had passed since sunup and the battle had yet to commence. The Uché must strike soon, if they hoped to have any advantage. He sent the signal forward to the troops under his command, and to the other battalion captains. Before the sun arose to its next glory, they would spill Otī and Sanguë blood.

Moving from their exalted positions, they readied to strike, though no enemy greeted them. Wary of a trap, they skulked forward with trepidation, watching all sides. *The Otī have forsaken the high ground completely!* Fola resisted sending more men to the forefront until it became obvious that the enemy could not take advantage of them. The other commanders sent more and did not hesitate. They drew closer and closer until a number of them paused and looked to the sky. An enlarged profile of the object many of them wore around their necks was positioned on a cliff above them.

"Behold, your Deliverer!" shouted Kaizari from a lower precipice. The distant image of Chimelu writhing upon the Revelation Gate inspired confusion among the ranks. *Is not Mkombozi supposed to enter the Revelation Gate? It was not a door, but a device of torture? Should not it have overturned the order?* Murmurs arose from whispers to audible complaints. Those with renewed faith in *Njia* began to doubt. *Shall we drop our weapons and surrender? Is there hope?*

Near the front of the brigades, Fola scaled the highest boulder he could find and whistled for their attention, threatening those who continued to spread rumors.

"Indeed, we have waited for *Mkombozi* for 800 years," he bellowed. "It was foretold *Mkombozi* was to start a New Order by entering the Revelation Gate. If *that* is the Revelation Gate, and he is *Mkombozi*, has he not entered it? Did he not raise me, and my men, from the dead? Did he not do what it would be prophesied that *Mkombozi* would do?

"Whether you believe he is *Mkombozi* or not, one thing you must agree upon – he has kept his word and his charge. He is still one of our own and our enemy makes sport of him. Have they not done so to us long enough? Must they slaughter *more* of our children or send our wives out as harlots before we take up arms? They spit upon the legacy of the Uché. Lay down your weapons, if you so choose, but I will not be denied freedom any longer! A New Order is at hand!"

A thunderous roar rumbled throughout the land, drawing the attention of Kaizari and Muuaji.

"On this day, our legacy shall be revised to read of our resounding victory over the Otī. Those who survive will remember the name of the Uché forevermore. Take up your arms and wage war. For *Mkombozi!* For *Mkombozi!*"

Proclaiming "For *Mkombozi!*" the Uché rushed forward into battle.

# TWENTY

## THE FIRST DAY OF FLOOD SEASON, 21 YEARS INTO ENSLAVEMENT, 23 A.B.

Though the Otī and Sanguë forces outnumbered those of the Uché, the latter drove them into temporary retreat with a furious assault on the front line and aerial support from the high places. After stripping the dead of their armor and weapons, to the delight of Kaizari, the battalions commanded by Fola proceeded forward. He and Muuaji observed the fight from a precipice, with Kaizari's threescore and six men idle behind them.

"These fools think they overcome us."

"What is to come next?"

Kaizari pointed to a treacherous part of the plain, where jagged rocks and thorned bushes forced the travel path to bottleneck.

"Once they reach there, we will decimate most of their strength. Your troops will circle around them and block the path of retreat. Mine will advance and trample them underfoot. From there, your army will overtake the rest and destroy them all. Then, EL will be summoned and conquered."

"If all of the slaves are destroyed, who then will we rule?"

Kaizari laughed heartily. "*We*? You shall rule nothing, not even in *Kuzimu*, where your soul will reside. You replacing me and ruling this realm *yourself*? Your thoughts betray you. If you believed this war was always about you, and your little nation of slaves, then you truly have been misled."

At that, he thrust a knife in between the joints of Muuaji's armor. The king collapsed to the ground and quickly perished. Kaizari reclaimed his blade, stepped over the lifeless body and ordered his men down to the battlefield.

Isoke tried not to stare at her son's beaten, naked body, but found it difficult to ignore the compassion and resolve in his eyes. He had raised his people from the dead, and she wondered why he did not heal his own wounds and descend from the Revelation Gate. *The pain he must be in!* It occurred to her that if he could, he would have rescued himself and fought alongside his people. Instead, he suffered for reasons she could not comprehend at all.

"Mama," he uttered, breathlessly. "Mama."

Isoke drew as close to the Revelation Gate as the sentries would allow. "Ask, and it shall be done for you."

"Make haste and leave me."

Isoke clutched her heart. "Ask anything else of me, Chimelu, but I shall not leave you until you descend from that atrocity."

Chimelu wheezed and coughed. "Survival depends on your obedience."

"No, it shall not be. I will not leave you again, not like this."

Chimelu looked to his left at Lusala, who rushed to Isoke's side. "Mama Isoke, do as he asks. What is it that must be done?"

Isoke's and Chimelu's eyes met. "You know where to go. And you will know what to do when you arrive there."

The words sent a chill through Isoke's soul. Hawa spoke the very same words to her before Chimelu's conception. She thought she might have died, but obeyed. To Chimelu's satisfaction, Isoke knelt and palmed a stone in her hand to commemorate the moment. It was an unusually dark copper color. Her vision blurred by tears, she bowed before him. *"Tazama Mkombozi."*

Lusala and Bimnono joined Isoke in worshipping him on her knees. Lusala vowed to hold onto this sight until her eyes closed and she rested with her ancestors. The first to stand, she kissed her fingers and held them toward Chimelu. Isoke rose.

"Be well," she said, "and I will see you, if the sun chooses to wake." Bimnono did the same.

The trio hastened down the approach and skulked under the cover of thorned vegetation and rock terrain around the Otī and Sanguë forces preparing to enter the battle. Though they did so covertly, a misstep by Lusala revealed their location to a young woman sent to provide victuals. She looked to be a concubine of the king. The girl paused, mouthed the names "Penda" and "Sifa," and held a finger to her lips. Not only did she keep the information from the men, but signaled them when the way was clear for them to proceed. *EL must be on our side,* they thought.

The Uché succeeded in their goals to cut down on the enemy numbers, secure more weapons and armor, and hold the advantageous positions. Still, Fola felt unsettled in his soul. After all, mathematically and tactically, they should have failed and fallen to the enemy. Now, they approached a portion of the land too narrow for a full company front to enter. It would have to be split into a fraction and enter in waves. He delayed the decision as long as possible, before messengers from the other leaders petitioned him for an immediate answer.

"Send three phalanxes down first. Split them accordingly and report the conditions to me. Tell the others to await my command."

Fola peered down into the deserted area where the men would advance. Per his orders, a trio of phalanxes pressed forward through the terrain. They paused at the opening to the other side and he could not gain a clear view of why they hesitated. The Uché released a battle cry and the front line charged. Suddenly, a cloud of black sand blew back in the direction of the troops at the rear. Soon, Fola gained a clear view. A small collection of giant soldiers advanced, brandishing swords and spears the likes of which had never been seen in this realm. With each powerful flourish, the Uché on the receiving end dissipated into piles of coarse grains.

"Retreat!" Fola cupped his hands at his mouth and yelled it in every direction. For those already engaged, they could not escape quickly enough. The giants ran amok with their dark arts, destroying every living thing in their path – even leveling rock and igniting thorned bushes. Soon, they turned their attentions to the entire Uché force. Arrows and spears slung from a distance fell harmlessly to the ground before having a chance to strike their targets. Their weapons knew little limits, slaying those they never came close to touching, nor drew within a stone's throw of reaching.

Odion and Ochen were among those behind the slaughter and hid in adjoining narrow clefts that the executioners would have to pass. They strung their bows and would fire as many times as possible before their certain destruction. The first arrows struck the unprotected necks of two of the soldiers. Unfazed, they plucked the arrowheads from beneath their skin like annoyances and did not break stride. The brothers waited until the threat passed before exiting. Their only hope was to flee.

The muscles in Chimelu's shoulders ached and cramped from the sustained upward position of his arms, and he could do nothing to lighten the pressure as the poles through his feet prevented it. Fire burned in his throat, chest and lungs, and each labored breath compounded it. The midday heat coaxed sweat from his pores, which dribbled into his open wounds and stung like a thousand bees. He repressed the urge to urinate until he could hold it no longer, drawing laughter from the attending guards.

For a moment, they turned their attention away from him and towards the battle, where Kaizari's threescore plus six devastated legions of the Uché in less than a movement of the sun. Wavering in and out of consciousness, Chimelu's head nodded.

"Awaken, brother." Zarek appeared before the Revelation Gate, twirling his finger. At his command, the poles through Chimelu's hands and feet rotated.

"I have no brother," Chimelu grimaced.

"But you do, Son of EL. I am the elder, of course, but kin, nonetheless." Zarek waved his hand, and the battlefield came into view through the cliff's surface. "Your people die by the legion. Soon, all that will remain is sand to fertilize the earth."

The scene brought sympathy to Chimelu's heart. He struggled to release himself from the Revelation Gate, but its binds constrained him.

"All this will come to pass, unless you join us. Lead them with me against EL. Once your people die, we will challenge him once more. You will rule at my right hand, second to only me in command."

Chimelu thoughts turned to Isoke, Lusala, Bimnono, Fola, Odion and Ochen. Zarek perceived his feelings. "They will all die miserable deaths. . .every last one of them," he said. "Join me."

"It cannot be," Chimelu responded. "Flee from me."

"Then let it begin." An angered Zarek disappeared in a puff of smoke and was transported to the front of the enemy lines. There, he uttered a proclamation in an unknown language. Lightning broke through the clear skies, and the earth shook at its foundation. Otī warriors of old dug themselves free from out of the ground around the soldiers – at the high places, in the valleys and beneath the feet of the Uché.

"Go forth," Zarek commanded, "and destroy the people of EL!"

Fola engaged the two demon soldiers next to him, dispelling their blows with his sword. Each fought with the strength of five men and the struggle greatly wearied him. He created an opening for himself and escaped, dodging any armed man in sight, enemy or not – even passing Odion and Ochen. The brothers did the same, but the trio soon found themselves surrounded. Many of their countrymen had fallen in that spot, as the surface felt and looked like the eroded silt left behind by the District River. All three thought to drop their weapons and surrender, but the disposition of their opponents did not bear the appearance of mercy or an interest in leaving survivors.

"For *Mkombozi!*" Fola yelled, and charged forward.

"How long must we be on this duty?" asked one of the sentries guarding Chimelu. "He does nothing besides mutter in his language and bleed to death."

"Until he perishes," answered the other. "Then, we are to deliver his body to the king. Would you defy the king's orders?"

"To be down there in the heat of battle? You would not?" The men shared a laugh. "Come. At least we can mock him until we tire of it again."

The guards turned from the battlefield to the Revelation Gate, which was empty and cracked in half. The spikes, which formerly bound Chimelu to the metal brackets and were bent to prevent removal, were straightened, wiped clean, and laid neatly beside one another on the ground. Frightened by what the emperor would do them for allowing this, they fell on their swords.

Both Lusala and Bimnono vomited at the edge of the Valley of Bones, for bodies had decomposed there for at least a moon. Though they covered their noses and mouths with cloths, they must do what Chimelu sent them there to accomplish. Lusala poked Isoke at the elbow, which confused the elder Uché. "It is not for me to do, Mama Isoke, it is for *you*. Have faith and believe in what you do."

The longer she hesitated, the worse the anticipation grew. Isoke uncovered her face, and thrust her hands to the skies, yelling "*Simama Uché!*" which means "Stand, Uché!"

For moments, nothing happened. A small seed of doubt pricked at Isoke, but she quelled it, fingering the stone in her pocket. Then, in one of the piles of bones, she saw movement – a hand digging for freedom. Over in another area, she heard the clatter of bones, and in another, a fully-restored and armed soldier. Too amazed with wonder, neither Isoke nor Lusala or Bimnono realized that the stench had completely dissipated.

In no time, men, women, and children crawled free from the Valley of Bones in never-ending waves. These were no puppets – they moved with clear purpose and intention. Even the women and children assumed the posture to fight, but they awaited something. Mosi's eleven brothers, dressed in the manner of clerics, came forth with Auni. Hawa appeared, completely restored and armed. They recognized Aitan, Madiha, Sakina, and Gamba, who had grown to maturity. The last to crawl free from the Valley of Bones was a soldier no greater in stature or build than the other men, but he distinguished himself with an almost regal air. He raised an imposing sword in the air and pointed it toward the battlefield.

"For *Mkombozi!*" The hordes made haste, running toward the war faster than any heard of oxen or cattle Isoke had ever seen. She smiled at Bimnono and Lusala, who shed a tear. Chimelu was almost certainly dead.

Fola, Odion and Ochen wallowed in agony, as these soldiers were flesh and blood, like them, and therefore sought to kill them in a traditional manner. All were struck through to the ground by spears and made to suffer.

For Fola, dying twice was more than he wished to

experience – especially in a manner similar to that of the first. The joviality of his enemies angered him, almost making the pain in his chest tolerable. In fact, he barely felt it anymore. He grasped the spear at its shaft and, to his surprise, pulled it from his chest without struggle. Using his right hand, Fola propped himself up to a sitting position and reclaimed his sword. Slowly, his strength and a renewed ability to breathe returned. Behind him, Odion and Ochen recovered, as well. Without question or comment, they sprung upon the Otī and killed them all. Odion faced the leader, who was one of the giants, and thrust a spear at his gut. The weapon struck true and sent him to his knees. Ochen sidestepped · his brother and beheaded the enemy.

They looked at one another, then at Fola. *What has happened to us? Have we truly cheated death?* The trio rejoined the battle, which resumed its previous course, but the Uché force had multiplied times upon itself. A confused Odion and Ochen jumped into the fray and found fighting came to them with ease. When the Otī retreated, a wave of soldiers pounced upon them and left no survivors. Even those who Zarek had raised from the ground fell and returned to the dust, while those Uché who fell at their sword revived and did battle. Fola noticed the peculiarity of the last man to exit the Valley of Bones and fought alongside the man to question him.

"Name yourself, friend."

"I am called Mosi," he said, extending his hand.

Instead, Fola saluted him, and the two of them hastened to the lone Otī general still standing, a man by the name of Kaizari. He had succeeded in fending off the Uché thus far, and now fought for his life, only able to keep the legions at bay. Mosi led Fola and the eleven plus Auni to the forefront, where they stood before Kaizari. The attacks ceased at the appearance of the old Uché king, who commanded the attention of even those who did not know of his importance.

"No, it cannot be," Kaizari said. "I watched you perish and now you stand before me?"

"It is finished, Kaizari. Lay down your arms."

"It has only begun. Where is your *Mkombozi*? I do not see him?"

"Where is *your* master?" Mosi challenged. "Bring him forth, that he may die alongside his most faithful servant."

Kaizari summoned *Adui wa EL* in all the manners he could, even by cursing him, but nothing manifested. Mosi hesitated no longer and struck a death blow. At Kaizari's falling, the soldiers rejoiced and celebrated the victory over the enemy. Sensing Fola's confusion over recent events, Mosi pulled him to the side.

Fola nodded. "Some of them were destroyed."

"You are mistaken. My brothers only recorded those which needed revelation to the people," he explained. "Had our enemies known them all, they would not have helped to fulfill them."

Still confused, Fola listened and did not question. Mosi explained *Adui wa EL* was, in fact, a fallen herald named Zarek who commanded his threescore plus six fallen heralds and their legions against the Uché. When Chimelu entered the Revelation Gate, the New Order began. EL would deal with Zarek personally, in time.

"Will I see Chimelu again?"

"It is possible," said Mosi. "It depends on where you look for him."

Upon their return, Isoke, Bimnono and Lusala took cover inside a cave occupied by similarly displaced women and children. Lusala took to comforting them, while Isoke, who fetched a discarded sword, stood guard at its entrance. A familiar voice called her name from behind.

"What has happened?" Mairi asked above the noise of dueling weapons. "We have been here since the fighting started, and have no idea what has happened."

"Chimelu entered the Revelation Gate," she admitted proudly, "and the tide is turning in our favor."

They remained until the peak of the day's heat passed and it started to rain. The war had passed them. They emerged, confident of their safety. Mairi extended her hand to Isoke, who took it. The two embraced. All was forgiven. Lusala wrapped her arms around them both. A young mother swaddling a newborn did likewise. Soon, the entire group exchanged warmth, pleasantries and tears.

They had survived.

Hand-in-hand, Lusala, Isoke, Bimnono and Mairi ascended to the moist surface. Face down in the soil, were myriads of Otī soldiers as far as the eye could see.

In the distance, an object resembling a large bird whisked into the sky and disappeared between the rain clouds. Lusala cast a knowing glance at Isoke, who cried tears of joy.

**THE END**

# A SHORT GLOSSARY OF UCHÉ TERMS

**A.C.:** "After Captivity" the epoch designating the number of years that have passed since the Otī overtook the Uché kingdom

**A.B.:** "After Birth" the epoch designating the number of years that have passed since the birth of *Mkombozi*

**Flood Season:** the flooding of the District River that occurs during the first four months of the Uché calendar; in modern times from the end of June until the end of October. It follows five days of feasting to celebrate the New Year.

**Harvest:** the period following the flooding season; in modern times, from the end of October to the end of February.

**Kusini mwa watu:** Kaizari's soldiers, consisting of 66 men over 800 years old.

**Kuzimu:** a place where EL condemned those who did not worship him.

**Maafa:** *a* disaster of the worst kind

**Moon:** the time between the appearing of a new moon, approximately 29 days

**Njia:** an invisible, phenomenal power native to only those of Uché blood

**Njia ya kifo:** an invisible, phenomenal power contrary to that of *Njia*; can be mastered by Otī, Sanguë, or Uché

**Simama:** "Arise!"

**Summer:** from the end of February to the middle of June; it precedes five days of feasting to celebrate the New Year.

**Tazama Mkombozi:** *"Behold, the Deliverer"*

# The Revelation Gate

## Book Club Study Guide

Finishing a novel feels like the end of a glorious marathon for me. Afterwards, I love thinking about what entertained or saddened me, and discussing the psychology behind the characters' behaviors with people who have read the same book. I sincerely hope these questions spark your group to have lively thoughts and conversations about the themes, issues, and conflicts at the heart of *The Revelation Gate*.

If you would like me to sit in on your group's discussion of *The Revelation Gate*, (in person or by phone) feel free to e-mail me at brian@brianlthompson.co

## GENERAL QUESTIONS

1. Which moments caught you by surprise?

2. The fates of a few characters, specifically Aitan, Kaizari, and Zarek, are unresolved. What do you think happened to them?

3. What is the book's strongest theme?

4. Put yourself in the writer's chair. How would you have ended the book?

5. The ultimate fate of *Mkombozi* is intentionally left open to interpretation. What do you think happened to him?

# CHARACTER SPECIFIC QUESTIONS

## Chimelu

1. Due to his calling as The Deliverer, Chimelu was restricted from marriage, although the clerical order did not forbid matrimony as a rule. Do you believe that members of clergy should be married to avoid the temptation Chimelu faced? Why or why not?

2. Auni trained Chimelu not to allow access to that which will hurt him. What is the right approach to follow when it comes to keeping hurts from reoccurring?

3. In his hour of need, Chimelu called on Mlinzi, and Mlinzi did not come to rescue him. Why do you think EL left Chimelu unprotected inside the well?

4. It had been foretold that when Chimelu (as *Mkombozi*) entered The Revelation Gate, the world's order would turn over. How did the Uché people change during the overthrow?

## Isoke:

1. Isoke married Aitan out of a promise Mairi bound her to keep. Point to specific events in the book that indicate she may have had romantic feelings for her husband.

2. Hawa verbally abuses Isoke during her teenage years because of her blood disease. Discuss instances you know of where a parent provoked their son or daughter because of a physical condition he/she could not control.

3. Though she knew of the prophecies, Isoke struggled to give her son over to Auni so that he could be trained in *Njia*. How would you have to be convinced to make that sort of sacrifice?

4. Explain the significance of the odd-colored stone that causes Isoke to stumble in Chapter Two and compare/contrast it with the significance of the stone she picks up while visiting Chimelu in the Revelation Gate.

### *Fola:*

1. Fola knew that Hawa had been committed to the hut for the mentally ill for some time. Discuss what you believe his reasoning was in keeping this knowledge from Isoke.

2. The underground militia of the Uché started to distrust Fola because he was reluctant to attack the Otī the way Letsego suggested. What effect do you think this had on him, as a man and a warrior?

3. In contrast to his sister, Fola's faith in *Mkombozi* seems to grow after Chimelu heals his wound. Why do you think Fola's response is different than that of his sister?

### *Lusala:*

1. Although her mother was half-Uché and her father was a full-blood Uché, Lusala was still considered Sanguë and looked down upon by the people in Nozi. If you, or someone you know, had a similar experience, describe what it is like to be mixed and treated as an outcast.

2. Lusala falls in love with Chimelu, who is forbidden

to marry her, and, in several instances, to touch her. Discuss what emotions she must have felt after being spurned by Chimelu.

3. Even before the vision Chimelu showed her, Lusala did not hesitate to believe in him. Why do you think her response was different than the majority of the Uché?

## Bimnono:

1. Why do you believe the relationship between Bimnono and Isoke is initially hostile?

2. Once a voluptuous dancer, Bimnono took pride in her physical appearance. After she bore Lusala, however, she could not slim down again. As this was her lone source of pride, how did this development affect her self-esteem?

3. After Isoke's attack, Bimnono said, "You cannot let evil lie! You have to cut off its head so it does not return." Discuss instances in which you believe this to be true or false.

## Letsego:

1. Letsego has several motivations for betraying his people, and his brother unto death. What are they?

2. Isoke is the object of Letsego's affection, though she is married to his brother and suffers a blood disease that renders her unclean. Why do you think he holds such attraction for her?

3. Letsego functions as spy to both Kgosi and his son, Kgosi II ("Muuaji"). How do you think he escaped suspicion of treason for so many years?

## *Muuaji:*

1. Muuaji has a temper and a violent disposition, considerably worse than that of his father. Discuss whether or not you believe his behavior was inherited from his father, or was a product of how he was raised.

2. Frustrated by growing political threats, Muuaji opted to enslave the Uché, who did not appear openly hostile until he did so. What are other ways he could have secured his rule without oppressing others?

3. Like his father, Muuaji often slept with Penda, an Uché concubine, before making major decisions and employed an Uché soldier, Kabal, as their chief guardsman. Why do you think Muuaji placed members of a race he hated in positions of importance?

9 780615 443744